THE EXPLORER

THE
EXPLORER

Katherine Rundell

Simon & Schuster Books for Young Readers

NEW YORK • LONDON • TORONTO • SYDNEY • NEW DELHI

SIMON & SCHUSTER BOOKS FOR YOUNG READERS
An imprint of Simon & Schuster Children's Publishing Division
1230 Avenue of the Americas, New York, New York 10020

Originally published in Great Britain in 2017 by Bloomsbury Publishing Plc

For information about special discounts for bulk purchases, please contact Simon & Schuster Special Sales at 1-866-506-1949 or business@simonandschuster.com.
The Simon & Schuster Speakers Bureau can bring authors to your live event. For more information or to book an event, contact the Simon & Schuster Speakers Bureau at 1-866-248-3049 or visit our website at www.simonspeakers.com.
Jacket design by Lizzy Bromley
Interior design by Hilary Zarycky
The text for this book was set in ITC New Baskerville Std.
Manufactured in the United States of America
1017 FFG

2 4 6 8 10 9 7 5 3
CIP data for this book is available from the Library of Congress.
ISBN 978-1-4814-1945-1
ISBN 978-1-4814-1947-5 (eBook)

To Charles

THE EXPLORER

Flight

LIKE A MAN-MADE MAGIC WISH, THE AIRPLANE began to rise.

The boy sitting in the cockpit gripped his seat and held his breath as the plane roared and climbed into the arms of the sky. Fred's jaw was set with concentration, and his fingers followed the movements of the pilot beside him: fuel gauge, throttle, joystick.

The airplane vibrated as it flew faster, following the swerve of the Amazon River below them. Fred could see the reflection of the six-seater plane, a spot of black on the vast sweep of blue as it sped toward Manaus, the city on the water. He brushed his hair out of his eyes and pressed his forehead against the window.

Behind Fred sat a girl and her little brother. They had the same slanted eyebrows and the same brown skin, the same long eyelashes. The girl had been shy, hugging her parents until the last possible moment at the airfield; now she was staring down at the water, singing under her breath. Her brother was trying to eat his seat belt.

In the next row, on her own, sat a pale girl with blond hair down to her waist. Her blouse had a neck ruffle that came up to her chin, and she kept tugging it down and grimacing. She was determinedly not looking out the window.

The airfield they had just left had been dusty and almost deserted, just a strip of tarmac under the ferocious Brazilian sun. Fred's cousin had insisted that he wear his school uniform, and now, inside the hot airless cabin, Fred felt like he was being gently cooked inside his own skin.

The engine gave a whine, and the pilot frowned and tapped the joystick. He was old and soldierly, with brisk nostril hair and a gray waxed mustache that seemed to reject the usual laws of gravity. He touched the throttle, and the plane soared upward, higher into the clouds.

It was almost dark when Fred first began to worry. The pilot began to belch, first quietly, then violently and repeatedly. His hand gave a sudden jerk, and the plane dipped drunkenly to the left. Someone screamed behind Fred. The plane lurched away from the river and over the canopy.

Fred stared at the man; he was turning the same shade of gray as his mustache. "Are you all right, sir?" he asked.

The pilot grunted, gasped, and wound back the throttle, slowing the engine. He gave a cough that sounded like a choke.

"Is there something I can do?" asked Fred.

Fighting for breath, the pilot shook his head. He reached over to the control panel and cut the engine. The roar ceased. The nose of the plane dipped downward. The trees rose up.

"What's happening?" asked the blond girl sharply. "What's he doing? Make him stop!"

The little boy in the back began to shriek. The pilot grasped Fred's wrist, hard, for a single moment; then his head slumped against the dashboard.

And the sky, which had seconds before seemed so reliable, gave way.

The Green Dark

FRED WONDERED, AS HE RAN, IF HE WAS dead. *But,* he thought, *death would surely be quieter.* The roar of the flames and his own blood vibrated through his hands and feet.

The night was black. He tried to heave in breath to shout for help as he ran, but his throat was too dry and ashy to yell. He jabbed his finger in the back of his tongue to summon up spit. "Is anybody there? Help! Fire!" he shouted.

The fire called back in response; a tree behind him sent up a fountain of flames. There was a rumble of thunder. Nothing else replied.

A burning branch cracked, spat red, and fell in a cascade of sparks. Fred leaped away, stumbling backward into the dark and smacking his head against something hard. The branch landed exactly where he'd been standing seconds before. He swallowed the bile that rose in his throat and ran faster.

Something landed on Fred's chin, and he yelled and ducked, smacking at his face and swerving into a bush; but it was only a raindrop.

The rain came suddenly and hard. It turned the soot and sweat on his hands to something like tar, but it began to quench the fire. Fred slowed his run to a jog, then to a stop. Gasping, choking, he looked back the way he had come.

The little airplane was in the trees. It was smoking, sending up clouds of white and gray into the night sky.

Fred stared around, dizzy and desperate, but he couldn't see or hear a single human, only the fernlike plants growing around his ankles, and the green trees reaching hundreds of feet up into the sky, and the panicked dive and shriek of birds. He shook his head, hard, trying to banish the shipwreck roar in his ears.

The hair on his arms had singed, and smelled of eggs. He put his hand to his forehead; the hair of his eyebrow had charred, and part of it came away on his fingers. He wiped his eyebrows on his shirt, noticing for the first time that his hands were covered in blood.

Fred looked down at himself. His trouser leg had

been ripped all the way up to the pocket, but none of his bones felt broken. There was vicious pain, though, in his back and neck, and it made his arms and legs feel far off and foreign. He picked up a stick and bit down on it; it was what they did during cross-country running at school. It helped, but only an infinitesimal amount.

A voice came suddenly from the dark. "Who's there? Get away from us!"

Fred spun around. His ears still buzzing, he grabbed a rock from the ground and hurled it in the direction of the voice. He ducked behind a tree and crouched on his haunches, poised to jump or to run.

His heart sounded like a one-man band. He tried not to exhale.

The voice said, "For God's sake, don't!"

It was a girl's voice.

Fred looked out from behind the tree. The light of the moon filtered deep green to the forest floor, casting long-fingered shadows against the trees, and he could see only two bushes, both of them rustling.

"Who is it? Who's there?" The voice came from the second bush.

Fred squinted through the dark, feeling the hair rise up on his arms.

"Please don't hurt us," said the bush. The accent was not British; it was something softer, and definitely a child, not an adult. "Was it you throwing poo?"

Fred looked down at the ground. He had snatched up a piece of years-old, fossilized animal dung.

"Oh," he said. "Yes." He was becoming accustomed to the dark. He could see the shine of eyes, peering out from the gray-green gloom of undergrowth. "Are you from the plane? Are you hurt?"

"*Yes*, we're hurt! We fell out of the sky!" said one bush, as the other said, "No, not badly."

"You can come out," said Fred. "It's only me here."

The second bush parted. Fred's heart gave a great leap. Both the girl and her brother were covered in scratches, in burns, and in ash—which had mixed with sweat and rain and made a kind of paste on their faces—but they were alive. He was not alone. "You survived!" he said.

"Obviously we did," said the first bush, "or we'd be less talkative, wouldn't we?" The blond girl stepped out into the driving rain. She stared from Fred to the other two, unsmiling. "I'm Con," she said. "It's short for Constantia, but if you call me that, I'll kill you."

Fred glanced at the other girl. She smiled

nervously, and shrugged. "Right," he said. "If you say so. I'm Fred."

"I'm Lila," said the second girl. She held her brother on her hip. "And this is Max."

"Hi." Fred tried to smile, but it made the cuts on his cheek stretch and burn, so he stopped, and made do with a grin that involved only the left half of his face.

Max was at the breathless stage of crying, and he clung to his sister so tightly his fingers were pressing bruises in her skin. She was leaning far over to the other side to hold him up, shaking with the effort. They looked, Fred thought, like a two-headed creature, arms entwined.

"Is your brother badly hurt?" he asked.

Lila patted her brother desperately on the back. "He won't talk—he's just crying."

Con looked back toward the fire and shivered. The flames cast a light on her face. She was, Fred saw, no longer blond. Her hair was gray with soot and brown with blood, and there was a scratch on her shoulder that looked deep.

"Are you all right?" he asked. He wiped rain out of his eyes. "That cut looks bad."

"No, I'm not all right!" Con spat. "We're lost, in

the Amazon jungle, and statistically speaking it's very likely that we're going to die."

"I know." Fred did not feel he needed reminding. "I meant—"

"So no." Con's voice grew thin and high. "I think it would be safe to say that none of us is all right, not at all, not even slightly!"

The bushes rustled. The rain hammered down on Fred's face.

"We need to find shelter," he said. "A big tree, or a cave or something that would—"

"No!" Max gave a sudden scream, a yell that was wet with spit and fear.

Fred stepped backward, raising his hands. "Don't cry! I just thought—" Then his eyes followed Max's pointing finger.

There, three inches from Fred's shoe, was a snake.

It was speckled brown and black, patchworked to match the jungle floor, and its head was as big as a fist. For one second nobody breathed. The jungle waited. Then Max let out a second scream that dug deep into the night, and the four of them turned and fled.

The ground was sodden and they ran pell-mell, sending mud up into one another's eyes, grazing their elbows against trees. Fred ran as if his body were not his own, faster than he'd ever run, his palms stretched ahead of him in the dark. Twice he tripped over a root and scrambled up, spitting earth. The rain blinded them. Shadows flashed past them in the darkness.

There was a yell behind him.

"Please, Max!" said Lila.

Fred turned back, skidding in the mud.

"He won't run!" Lila bent over her brother in the mud. "And I can't carry him!"

The little boy lay on his back, weeping up at the sky, his whole body shaking in the driving rain.

"Come on!" Fred bent and heaved Max over his shoulder. The boy was far heavier than he'd expected, and he screamed as Fred lifted him, but Fred grabbed both of Max's knees and started running, his whole body screaming with pain. He could hear Lila, her feet thumping close behind them.

The stitch in Fred's side was almost unbearable when he tore out of the trees and into a sudden clearing. He halted, and Max bumped his head against Fred's spine and yelled. Angrily, he began trying to bite one of Fred's shoulder blades.

"Please don't," said Fred, but he was barely paying

attention to the boy on his back. He stared, stunned and breathless, ahead of him.

They stood in the middle of a wide circle of trees, open to the sky and lit by the fat moon. There was a carpet of green moss and grass, and the stars above them were clustered so thickly that the silver outnumbered the night. Fred lowered Max to the ground and stood bent over, his hands on his thighs, panting.

"Did the snake chase us?" said Max.

"No," gasped Con.

"How do you know?" wailed Max.

Lila dropped to her knees, clutching at her side. "Snakes don't chase, Maxie. We both know that. I just . . . forgot."

"We panicked," said Con. Her voice was bitter. "That's what happened. See! Look: no snakes. We were stupid. Now we're even more lost."

Fred stared around. The ground in the clearing sloped slightly downward, toward a large puddle of water. He crossed over to it, his muscles aching, and sniffed; it smelled of rotting things, but he was feverishly thirsty. He took a tiny sip, and immediately spat it out. "No good," he said. "It tastes like a dead person's feet."

"But I'm thirsty!" said Max.

Fred looked around the clearing, hoping to find water before Max started crying again.

"If you wring out your hair," he said, "there'll be water in it." He tugged his dark hair down over his forehead, and twisted: A few drops fell on his tongue. "It's better than nothing."

Max chewed on his hair for a moment, then scrunched his eyes closed. "I'm scared," he said. It was said without whining: a simple matter of fact. Somehow, Fred thought, it was worse than the tears.

"I know," Lila said softly. "We all are, Maxie." She crossed to her brother and pulled him close to her. His small, bony fingers closed over a burn on her wrist, but she did not brush him away. She began to whisper in his ear in Portuguese: something soft, almost a song; a lullaby. Gently she picked the leaves and mud out of the scrapes on Max's arms and legs.

Fred looked at them. They were both shaking slightly. "All of this will look less bad in the morning," he said.

"Will it?" said Con. There was bite to the question. "Will it, really?"

"It can't look much worse," he said. "Once it's light, we'll be able to work out a way to get home."

Con looked hard at him; there was challenge in the look, and Fred stared unblinking back at her. Her face was all geometry: sharp chin, sharp cheekbones, sharp eyes.

"What now, then?" she said.

"Our mama and papa say—," began Lila. The mention of her parents made her face crease and convulse, but she swallowed and went on. "They always say: 'You need to sleep before you think.' They say: 'When you're exhausted, you do stupid things.' And they're scientists. So we should sleep."

Fred found his whole body was aching. "Good. Fine. Let's sleep."

He lay down on his side in the wet grass. His clothes were soaked through, but the air was warm. He closed his eyes.

Perhaps, he thought, he would wake up in his bed at school, next to the snoring of his roommates, Jones and Scrase. An ant crawled over his cheek.

"But aren't we supposed to stay awake in case we die of concussion?" said Con.

"I think if we'd got concussion, we'd be dizzy," said Lila.

Fred, already half asleep, tried to work out if he was

dizzy. The world began to spin away from him.

"If we all die in the night, I'm blaming both of you," said Con.

It was on that cheering thought that Fred felt himself dropping down, down, away from the jungle and the thick night air, and into sleep.

The Den

I T WAS FEROCIOUSLY HOT, AND HE WAS STILL alive. Those were the first thoughts that came to Fred as he opened his eyes and found himself staring straight up at the Brazilian sun. Instinctively, he looked down at his wristwatch, but the face was cracked and the minute hand had fallen off.

The two girls were asleep next to him. Both of them were covered in blood and scabs, but they were breathing easily. Con had her thumb in her mouth. There was a host of dragonflies, in luminous blues and reds, dancing around their clothes; they seemed, Fred thought, to be attracted to the blood.

But there was no sign of the little boy. Max was missing.

"Max!" Fred whispered, jumping to his feet. There was no answer, no movement except the burr of dragonfly wings.

Fred's heart started to pound. "Max?" he called louder. Lila stirred in her sleep.

He ran to the edge of the trees. There was no trace of the boy.

"Max!" he roared. He stared wildly around.

"What?" Max sat up; he had been lying on his stomach behind some fernlike plants next to the vile-smelling puddle, splashing his fingers in the water.

"Max!" Fred ran over to him, wincing as one of his ribs protested sharply. "You haven't been drinking that water, have you?"

Max stared up at Fred as he approached, then screwed his eyes shut and gave a scream that shook the baby flesh in his cheeks. Across the clearing, Lila yelled as she startled awake.

"That's not very flattering," said Fred. But it was possible, he reckoned, that covered in blood and soot, and with less eyebrow than usual, he did not look very reassuring.

The boy kept screaming, barely drawing breath. Lila jumped to her feet and stood staring across at them. "Max!" she called. "What's happened?"

Sugar, Fred thought. He knew that you should give people sugar for a shock. "Do you want a sweet?" He had had some mints in his pocket. "Please stop crying!" He fished the candy out.

His hand came out wet. There was a cut on his thigh and half-dry blood in his pocket, and the mints had spent the night marinating in it. He grimaced, and put one in his mouth. The taste had not been improved, but the sugar gave his blood a twitch.

"Do you want one of these?" Fred spat on a corner of his shirt and polished one clean. "It's a mint."

"No! I hate mints!" said Max.

"It's the only food I've got."

"Oh. Then I'll take it," said Max. He said it like a lord accepting a peasant's bread. As Max sucked loudly, his nose began to run, down past his lips and onto his chin.

"Max!" Lila called. "Come here!"

"Come on," said Fred. The boy's face was intent on working on the mint; it was such a small face, and so vulnerably soft. Fred felt his chest tighten. But he only said, "You should probably blow your nose."

"I don't blow my nose," said Max. They walked, both limping, toward Lila. "It's not a thing I do."

"I think you should."

"No!" Max licked the snot off his upper lip and added it to his mouthful of mint.

Five-year-olds, Fred thought, were not easy to argue with. Max had a sweep of dirt encrusted on his cheek, and his eyebrows turned up at the corners; it gave his face a mischievous tilt.

Fred hooked his finger into Max's shirt collar to steer him from thorns and piles of what looked like rabbit droppings. The ground was mossy, speckled with patches of grass and creeper. One of the trees had scarlet flowers, which had fallen and red-carpeted the forest floor.

Among the flowers, under the bright white sun, Lila and Con were arguing.

"You! Boy, whatsyourname, Fred!" called Con. "Come and tell this girl she's completely wrong."

"She thinks—," began Lila, flushing.

"Obviously, I think we should go back and wait near the plane," said Con. "In case they see it from the air. So they can rescue us."

"It makes more sense to stay here," said Lila. She pulled her knees up to her chin and looked down as she spoke. "We'd just get lost, trying to find our way back. And I don't think anyone will see the plane. They don't know where we crashed; they'll have to search the entire jungle. We're on our own." She fixed her eyes on a dandelion-like plant, fierce and unblinking. "We're going to have to find a way to get to Manaus ourselves."

Fred looked at the girl properly. She had a scratch up the side of her narrow face, and hair woven into two dark braids, one of which had been charred in the crash. She wore a scarlet skirt, and darker red top, now stained gray green. She looked about his age, or a little younger.

Con glared. "That's crazy. We need to stay near the plane and wait to be rescued. My family will have sent dozens of planes to search for us by now. A hundred planes, probably."

"But," said Lila, "where we crashed is burnt by the fire. Half the trees are charcoal, and so there'll be no animals—"

"We don't need animal friends!" said Con. "This isn't a fairy tale!"

"—for us to eat," finished Lila. "And back there, there's—"

"What?" said Con.

"There's the pilot."

"He's dead," said Con. She seemed genuinely puzzled. "He can't hurt us."

Lila spoke very quietly, but Fred was surprised by how authoritative she sounded. "We should make camp here."

"No!" said Con. "That's completely illogical."

"Fred?" asked Lila. "You get the deciding vote."

"No, he doesn't!" said Con. "That's not fair; one person shouldn't get to decide!" She glared at Fred, from foot to chin. "Not unless he agrees with me."

Fred looked around the clearing again. The air was fresh here, and the sky above them a blue that does not exist in England. He was just about to answer when he saw that at the far end, where the forest grew thick again, four trees had fallen together, their tops meeting in a point. Fred stared at them. The very tips of the hair on the back of his neck began to rise.

"Do you think there's anything odd about this clearing?" he said.

"That's not an answer to the question!" said Con.

"Why?" asked Lila.

"Those trees," said Fred, "over there." He pointed.

"What about them? They fell over," said Con. "That's what trees do."

"But they don't look like they fell, to me," said Fred. He ran across the clearing. A sense of something strange was rising up in him, and his curiosity pushed aside his fear.

The largest of the trees was immense: Its trunk was as thick and tall as the column in Trafalgar Square. Three smaller trees leaned against the thicker one. Each had grown up a few feet from the next in a rough square, and their branches were entwined and darkened by green creepers.

"Leave it alone, Fred," called Con. "Stay in the open!"

"There's something odd here." Fred ran his hand down one of the smaller trees. At the base was a mess of small fernlike plants and a few mushrooms. He pushed the ferns down, and felt his stomach swoop.

The three smaller trees did not have roots. They were logs, twenty feet high, each carefully leaned against the central tree; he could see where they had been hacked, with an ax or a machete. Ferns had grown—*or been planted,* Fred thought—at their base, disguising the place where the cut showed.

"A den," breathed Fred.

"What did you say?" called Con.

Fred pushed at the vines that stretched between the logs.

"It's like a tent," said Fred. "A den." He bent down, ready to push past the foliage.

"No! Don't go in there!" said Con. It came out in a burst. "It's not that I'm scared. But please don't. It's not a reasonable risk."

Fred stared at her. "A what?" He had never in his life considered whether a risk was reasonable; it sounded like something his headmaster would say.

"There could be anything in there! Jaguars, or snakes, or rats," said Con.

"I can't *not* look!" said Fred, astonished.

"She might be right, though, Fred," said Lila. "About the snakes. Be careful."

"*I'll* look!" said Max grandly, jumping to his feet.

"No, you absolutely won't!" said Lila, grabbing his wrist. "You're staying right here."

Fred pushed aside the vines hanging down from between the logs.

"Ach!" He winced: Some of the tendrils had tiny but vicious thorns, and he had to pause to pick them out of his skin. He brushed away another handful of vines, and stopped. His heart, which had not stopped foliage and pushing it outside. Underneath, the earth was soft and dusty; it smelled of a thousand warm days, layered one over the other.

Lila brought in an armful of leaves, each as big as a pillowcase. She began to lay them for beds.

"And we could hang some extra vines over the front of the den," said Fred, "so nothing can see in."

Con crouched in the shelter with her arms crossed. "Who died and made you king?" she asked.

"Nobody!" Fred turned, startled; he could feel himself flushing red hot. "But if we're going to sleep here, we might as well make it waterproof."

"I'm not sleeping here!" said Con. "Someone could come back here any second."

"But they won't," said Fred. "Did you see those flints?"

"Yes?"

"They're covered in moss," he said.

"So they're dirty. Fine. How is that supposed to be reassuring?" said Con.

"He means they're old," said Lila. "It's deserted."

"But why do you want to risk it?" said Con. "What if they come back and they think we're intruders?"

"Or what if they're never coming back, and they've

double-beating since the crash, quickened to triple speed.

The trees met to make a tent, high enough for a man to kneel in, or for someone Max's height to stand. The air smelled deep green. There was a spider's web in one corner; under it was a pile of banana leaves, spread out a dozen leaves thick in the shape of a sleeping mat. They had been almost entirely devoured by ants.

Fred looked up, and felt his eyes stretch wide. "Come and look at this!" he called. The space in between the four great tree trunks had once been covered in a roof of woven palm leaves. He reached up and touched them. The palms were riddled with holes, half rotted, and the light shone through, but he could see how intricately they had once been woven.

He crawled farther in, slowly, looking for snakes in the green light. The ground squelched under his hands. In the far corner of the den was a hollow gourd, rotten with mildew. Fred touched it, gingerly; it was mulchy. He turned it upside down, wrinkling his nose at the smell. A cascade of flints spilled out. Half were chipped to the shape of arrowheads; others were square and squat, large as a fist.

"You two!" He crawled backward and stuck his head through the vines. "Come in! Quick, you have to see this! Someone was here!"

"You're crazy!" spat Con. "If someone was here, they won't want us trespassing! I've had enough of this." She turned and began to march back into the trees.

"Wait! Con! We shouldn't split up!" called Fred. Infuriated, he scrambled out and ran after her.

"Whose house is it?" She turned to face him. Fred was startled to see there were tears in her eyes. "You don't know, do you?"

"Of course I don't," said Fred, "but I just think—"

"What if they come back? I've read about it, in . . ." Con hesitated, casting around for an idea. "Goldilocks. I know how it ends! I'm not getting eaten!"

"I'm pretty sure this place wasn't built by bears," said Fred.

"It could be cannibals!"

"Cannibals are mostly a myth," said Lila.

"Says who?"

"Everyone! Scientists! Our mama and papa."

"How do they know?"

"Mama grew up in the jungle, near the Solimões River. And she's a scientist. A botanist."

"Bottomist!" said Max.

Con scowled at him, her nerves twitc face. "You overrate the wit of the word 'bo

Lila put a protective arm around Max as if she hadn't been interrupted. "And English, and he studies the plants of the medicine. And our grandmother was assistant; we were supposed to be going to England. We were going to get the boat fro She wanted to meet us before she died; sh see what Max was like."

Con snorted. "Perhaps it's just as well we

Lila ignored that. "Listen! Whoever liv they come back—might able to take us to

"Or they could *eat us for dinner*," said looked from Lila to Fred, angry and bewild

"Just come inside," said Fred. "You'll see been here for ages."

Grudgingly, very slowly, Con turned ar bent and edged into the shelter. Lila and Ma

Fred pulled at the rotten leaves lining the could weave fresh leaves for the ceiling," he make new beds. Then it would smell less lik

He began gathering armfuls of half-de

left behind this shelter?" said Lila. Her voice was not loud, but it was strong. "If someone was here, that means someone else thought it was a good place to rest. It means it's safe."

"But you can't *know* for sure—"

"But we can't know anything for sure!" said Fred. "Lila's right. As soon as we work out how to get out of here, we'll leave. But until then, it makes sense to stay in a place where people have been."

"Unless they EAT US!" said Con.

"I'm staying here," said Max. "I want to live in the tree-tent. And if you try to make me move, I'll do a wee on you."

"No, you won't!" Con backed away, hitting the back of her head on the tree trunk.

"He does sometimes do that," said Lila.

Which, for the moment at least, more or less settled it.

The River

I T TOOK SOME TIME TO FIND LEAVES WIDE AND strong enough for the roof. The first batch Fred tried tore in his hands, and the second turned out to have something in them that made his skin turn red and itchy; but the third tree had fleshy leaves as long as his arm. He and Lila together tore them into strips and wove them into great squares, which they wedged in and out of the branches of the supporting trunks. Con sat on the grass outside the den, digging a hole in the ground with a twig.

Fred crawled into the den and looked up. The sun no longer filtered through a thousand ant holes. The light inside was dark green: an underwater, sunken-treasure color. He felt a battered kind of triumph surge through him.

"It works!" he called. "You can barely see the gaps."
He heard Lila cheer.

Fred backed out of the den and stood up too fast. Suddenly his head reeled, colors flashing in front of his eyes. His lungs tied in a double knot.

"Are you all right?" asked Lila.

"Fine," he said, more brusquely than he'd intended. Since his pneumonia he hated being asked if he was all right. He tried to smile. "Thanks," he added.

Fred had been sent to Brazil to recover, living with a distant cousin. The cousin's idea of a good time involved more playing bridge in a dark drawing room than Fred had expected. But, his father had said, it was the only sensible option.

"I can't be at home to look after you," he had said. "The firm needs me."

"I can look after myself," Fred had wheezed.

"That's not possible," Fred's father said gruffly. He had worked longer and longer hours each year, ever since Fred could remember. Fred could not remember his mother's face, except when he was asleep.

He had never seen his father dressed in anything other than a suit, and the suits seemed, over time, to have seeped into his father's skin. His voice practically wore a tie.

"You're treating me like a baby," Fred had said.

"Nonsense," his father had said. "Come on. You're a sensible boy."

Fred's boarding-school report always contained that word: "sensible." "An unobtrusive presence in the classroom." Sometimes, when they could clearly think of nothing else that distinguished him from his classmates: "increasingly tall."

Fred knew he was none of those things. Or rather: He was tall. Nobody would have argued about that; he grew out of clothes so fast that his ankles were constantly cold.

But he was not unobtrusive inside, nor was he sensible.

Inside, Fred was hunger and hope and wire. It was just that there had never yet been a chance to prove it; his father had always insisted so unswervingly on clean shoes and unrebellious eyebrows. But Fred's mind was quick, with sharp edges. He wanted more from the world than it had yet given.

Now he tried to grin at Lila. "I'm just dehydrated. We need to find something to drink," he said. "You can live for a long time without eating—"

"No, you definitely can't," said Max indignantly.

"—but you can't live for long without water."

"Do you think we can drink from the"—Lila hesitated, searching for the word—"tiny cesspool?"

Fred looked across at the puddle of water. "We *could*, but I don't think we'd live very long if we did. But we're near the river—we must be," he said.

"It was on our left when we crashed," said Lila eagerly.

"Which direction did we run?" said Con.

"Well, the sun rises in the east. So, facing this way, left is northeast," said Fred.

"How does that help, if we don't know which direction we ran?" snapped Con. She was pale, and there were circles under her eyes, as if someone had pressed a paint-smeared thumb to her face.

"It doesn't, much," admitted Fred. But northeast of here was England. The thump in his chest slowed a little: Northeast led to his bedroom at home, his bookcase, his cricket bat propped up against the wall. It led to his father.

Con squared her shoulders as if readying to fight. "Are we just going to guess, then?"

"I heard," Fred said, "that you can follow ants, and they'll take you to water."

"Ants!" said Con. "We're going to take directions from *ants*?"

Lila stared hard at Con, and then at the ground, combing the leaves with her eyes. "Do you have a different suggestion?" she said.

Con sighed, and bent to look under a log.

The first set of ants was a disappointment. Max found a trail of tiny red ones, and bent down to stroke them. "Look! They're shining!"

"Don't touch!" said Lila, snatching him back. "Some ants out here are dangerous."

"These ones?" asked Con, taking a step backward.

"I don't know, that's the problem! The dangerous ones are called bullet ants, but I don't know what they look like."

"Bullets, presumably," said Con.

"Not necessarily," said Lila. "Dogfish don't look like dogs. I remember being very disappointed."

"These ones just look like ants," said Max.

"You're still not allowed to touch them," said Lila. "So don't try."

So they walked at a safe distance, all four of them with their chins on their chests, along a snaking line of trees. The ants led them to a large pile of leaves.

"Oh." Fred nudged the leaves with a stick, just in case there was water underneath. He recoiled.

The ants were swarming over the carcass of a bird. It looked like it had, once, been a vulture. Now, though, it was equal parts bones and smell.

"That isn't exactly what I was hoping would happen." You could not, he thought, trust an ant's sense of priorities.

"What now, then?" asked Con. She crossed her arms.

"Let's try again," said Lila. "Maybe those were the wrong kind of ants."

It was Lila who found the trail of larger ants: ants with heads as big as ball bearings. They followed the track deep into the woods, Lila leading. Fred watched her. She was small and moved on the edge of her muscles, like an animal—a deer or a lemur—as if she heard things other people did not.

"I can't believe we're trusting ants," said Con. She brushed a cobweb out of her hair and ducked under a branch. "Even in fairy stories, it's a wise owl or something. Nobody goes to bloody ants for help." She looked defiantly at Fred as she said the word "bloody," and then a thorn caught on the skin above her eyebrow, and she let out a shriek. "I *hate* this place!"

Fred looked back and found, with a lurch to his stomach, that the clearing had entirely disappeared.

"Which way is the way back?" he said. The green of the forest seemed to thrum around them.

"Left at that tree that was covered in mushrooms, and then right at a bush with green thorns," said Con. She didn't look at him, didn't see the surprise on his face, which he immediately tried to hide.

"We should mark our way," he said, "so we can find our way back here."

"Fine," said Con. "Unless you want to ask the opinion of, I don't know, a passing maggot?"

Fred grinned. "Well, maggots are much slower walkers." She didn't smile back. He broke a branch and stuck a leaf on the hinge it made.

Con shook her head. "That's not going to be any good. You need something bigger." She tore one of the ruffles off her once-white blouse, and tied it to a tree. "There."

Fred turned to look at her, crouched in the dappled light. She moved stiffly, as if unaccustomed to her own body. And her clothes seemed to sit on her like a bear trap. There are outfits that suggest of their own accord that their owner should sit still and smile nicely. Con had been dressed in one such outfit, before the crash had colored it brown and green and red.

"Good thing you've got ruffles to spare," he said, and grinned.

Con gave him the kind of look that breaks noses. "You've only got half your eyebrows, so you can shut up."

"Sorry!" Fred stepped backward. "I only meant—it's useful, to have clothing with extra bits attached. Boys' clothes don't."

"Fine. Whatever you say. You don't have to try to be nice to me, you know."

"What?" Fred stared, bewildered.

"I just want to get out of this vile place, and get back to school. I don't mean to be rude, but I'm not really interested in making friends. Especially not with little kids."

Lila heard them. "I'm not a little kid," she said quietly. She spoke without taking her eyes off the ants. "I'm just small for my age."

"How old are you?" Con turned to Fred.

Fred told her.

"But that's hardly older than me!" said Con.

"And me," said Lila.

"I thought you were much older!" said Con.

Fred shrugged. "Just tall," he said.

"But that means there's no adults! Not even any nearly-adults. Just four children. In the Amazon jungle."

"That," said Fred, "sounds true."

"Unfortunately," said Lila.

"Un-fornatuely," echoed Max. He had wandered off a few paces, blowing nose-bubbles with his snot; Lila darted after him and grabbed him by the sleeve. "Stay close!" she said. Her face was bones and eyes and nerves.

As they walked on, a smell came to Fred on the air; something sharp and fresh, something that smelled more blue than green.

"Is that the river? I think I can smell it," he said.

"Don't be ridiculous," said Con. "You can't smell water—"

But then she broke off. Through the thickly ranged trees, Fred could see a flicker of something that moved.

"Come *on*!" called Con. "I've found the river!"

They stood where the ground curved down to meet the river. The river was a stark, bright blue.

"Do you think there are caiman?" Lila asked. Despite the sun overhead, she shivered.

In the long winter of Fred's illness, he'd read dozens of books about explorers, about men venturing out into the wild armed with a pith helmet and a penknife. He had a shelf full, all dog eared and food stained, and they all dwelled, at great length, on caiman.

He decided to be honest. "Probably," he said, "but I don't know where else we're going to get water."

"What are caiman?" asked Con.

"Alligators," said Fred. "Like crocodiles. But with longer snouts."

"But they're smaller," said Lila. "Probably."

"*Probably,*" said Con. "Oh, good."

"The caiman like the sunny sides of the bank," said Lila. "And we're in shade here. So we're *probably* fine."

"*Everything's* a risk here," said Fred. "I'm going in." Every hair on his arms stood on edge as he scanned the bank.

Fred pulled off his shirt, then put it back on again. It occurred to him that it needed washing as much as he did.

He slipped down the bank, his feet squelching in the mud, and dived in headfirst.

The river was a gift. It soothed the burn of his cuts and the ache in his feet. Fred trod water. He kicked downward, below the surface where it was colder, and sucked in a mouthful of water.

It had a tang of mud to it, and a strand of waterweed wrapped itself around his tongue, but at that moment it was the most delicious thing he had ever drunk: better than hot chocolate at Christmas or fresh lemonade in summer. "Come in!" he called.

Lila plunged in after him, carrying Max on her shoulders. Con hesitated on the edge, her face stiff and anxious.

"We didn't do swimming at school," she said. "Only ballroom dancing." She entered the water slowly and swam in a nervous doggie paddle, her chin high above the water.

Fred rubbed his arms and legs, feeling his cuts sting as he scrubbed the dirt off them, then kicked below the surface again, his eyes open in the dark water. A shoal of miniature fish swam by, followed by a single larger one. He came up for air.

"There's fish!" he called.

"Try to catch one!" called Con.

Fred plunged down again. The small fish darted away as he grabbed at them. The larger fish ignored him completely, but there was something eerie in its shape—almost circular, like a swimming dinner plate. The fish turned. It bared its teeth at him.

Fred sucked in a lungful of river water and shot, coughing, to the surface. "Piranhas!" he yelled. "Get out!"

Max was floating near him; Fred grabbed him and struck out for the bank, fear pounding through his limbs.

"What are piranhas?" Con asked.

"Fish with teeth!"

Con screamed a word Fred hadn't expected her to know, then swallowed a mouthful of water and disappeared under the surface.

Lila, wild-faced, grabbed her by the shoulders. "Don't thrash!" she said. She hooked one arm around Con's waist, kicking for the shore. "Just breathe!"

Fred and Max scrambled up the bank, Con and Lila just behind them. They lay, panting, on the hot earth.

Con let out a groan, and spat out a mouthful of weeds. "Fish! Fish with teeth! Nothing is safe here. You can't even trust the fish not to eat you. What else? Pigeons with fangs? Monkeys with guns?"

"I read," Fred gasped, "that they don't bite unless they're very hungry."

"They mostly eat small things. You know, birds and frogs," said Lila. She wrung out her hair. It was covered in a dusting of red-brown river silt.

"It looked"—Fred drew in a great breath, and felt his heart begin to slow—"like it wasn't going to do anything. It was actually quite beautiful. Silver with a red belly."

"Beautiful?" Con stared incredulously.

"As long as we're not bleeding into the water, we won't attract them," said Lila. "I knew that, but I panicked. We're still safe to swim here. I think they'll ignore us."

"You *think*! You think you think you *think*!" Con was red in the face, sharp boned. "They're fish with teeth! Piranhas! You can't *psychoanalyze* them!"

Lila looked at Con; her face was inscrutable. "I think," she said, "that the plural of piranha is piranha, not piranhas."

"Oh, good," said Con. "It's always nice to be grammatically correct when you're being eaten."

They padded, damply, back to the clearing. Lila used her wet shirt to wipe the mud off Max's face as they went. Their bodies steamed in the sun as they dried.

Coming back into the clearing felt surprisingly like coming home. A scarlet parrot alighted on a branch above Fred's head, cawed in surprise at the band of dripping children, and took off again.

Fred found the sharpest of the flints and hacked off the bottom of his gray school trousers, making them into rough-edged shorts. The left leg was longer than the right, but he decided it didn't matter. He rolled up the sleeves of his shirt.

Something in Fred was beginning to glow: under the sun, and the cry of the birds, and the expanse of vivid green around them. It was huge, and dizzying.

It felt like hope.

Either that, he thought, *or concussion.*

Food (Almost)

ALTHOUGH FRED HAD DRUNK SO MUCH water that the skin on his stomach was stretched tight, he was still painfully hungry. His insides ached and growled noisily. Fred thumped his front with a fist. His body felt at half-mast, weak and flimsily built.

He hadn't eaten anything since an apple before he'd boarded the airplane. He wasn't sure how long ago that was: a day and a half? He thought back: The flight had been on a Saturday, so today was probably—unless they'd all been unconscious for a long time—Sunday.

Fred shivered. He shook his head, trying desperately to clear the picture of the burning plane from behind his eyes. "I think there are insects we can eat," he blurted more to distract himself than anything else.

The comment was greeted with a silence so unenthusiastic that it seemed to have its own particular smell.

"And we can find fruit," he added. "There's got to be some. There are monkeys, and the monkeys have to be eating something. Bananas, maybe. There were banana leaves in the den. Or berries."

"How will we know if the berries are safe?" said Con.

"I'll test them," said Fred.

"What if you die?" asked Con.

"Maybe we all should test them. If we find any," said Lila. "But not Max."

"Why not?" said Con. "If we're risking our lives, why shouldn't he?"

"Because he's too young!" said Lila. "And he has allergies."

"That's not fair!" said Con. She smacked a small rock against a large one.

Fred could feel his own temper slipping away; the heat was burning, and his stomach felt bitter and tight. "Con," he said, "come on."

"You don't know me well enough to tell me to *come on*. Nobody voted you leader."

Fred bit his tongue, feeling his nostrils flare angrily. "I didn't say I was!"

Lila face was crumpling. "Don't." She swallowed, and tried to change the subject. "What were you saying about insects?"

"One of my books said you can eat the insects that eat cocoa pods."

"What book?"

"Just a book about explorers." It had been about Percy Fawcett, a man who had come to the Amazon in search of golden cities. It was the kind of book that left you breathless and eye stretched.

"What did your *book*"—Con pronounced the word with distrust—"say the insects look like?"

"Small," said Fred. "It said not to eat any insect too big to put up your nostril."

"Any further detail on that?" asked Con. Even her teeth looked sarcastic.

"No." Fred wished, not for the first time, that more of his books had had pictures.

"Lila will know," said Max proudly. "Lila knows all about animals. She nearly got expelled for trying to keep a squirrel in her desk." He grinned. "Mama was so angry."

"Shush, Max!" Lila glared, embarrassed, at her brother.

"Well, insects aren't animals!" said Con. "So none of this is useful."

"*Do* you know?" Fred asked Lila. There was a spark of something stirring behind her eyes.

"I'm not sure," said Lila. "But, actually—" She jumped to her feet. "Max—stay here. I'll be right back."

"What? No!" Max put down the leaf he was chewing on and screwed his face into an angry ball. "Wait!"

But Lila had gone, running out of the clearing, her half-burnt braids swinging behind her.

The fifteen minutes that followed were not peaceful. Max tried to follow Lila, but Lila had disappeared into the undergrowth and couldn't be found. Fred picked Max up to stop him from running out through the unmarked, thick-crowded trees. Max bit Fred on the back of the hand; Con called him a brat; Max bit Con on the shin.

Before Con could bite Max back, Lila burst out of the trees. Her eyes were raw with relief. "Thank goodness! I thought I was lost! I missed a turn somewhere," she said, her breath jagged edged. She had made her jersey into a kind of sack, held in both arms; her forehead was shining with sweat.

"Did you find food?" asked Con.

"Yes," she said. Then her honesty got the better of her and she added: "Almost."

She opened her improvised sack and poured dozens of pods onto the grass.

"They don't all have larva holes in them," she said. "But I thought we could eat the cocoa beans too." She began breaking them open with her nails.

Fred picked up one of the pods; there were two holes in the top. "There's something in here." He tried to shake the something out, but it didn't come. He poked a stick into the hole and shook it again, and a fat little grub, an inch long, tipped out onto his palm.

"That's it!" said Lila. "That's the grub! You can eat it!"

"Oh, good," lied Fred. The grub lay on his hand: It didn't move, but seemed to be pulsating slightly. He sniffed it.

"Go on," said Con. "It was your idea."

"Ugh." Fred pinched his nose, braced himself, and bit the grub in half. It was soft, but its insides were sandy, and the crunch of it against his teeth made him shudder. He swallowed with difficulty. "It tastes a tiny bit like chocolate," he said.

"*Really?*" said Con. Her whole face, and even her ears, were skeptical. It is difficult to make ears register emotion, but Con managed it.

"But mostly like dirt," Fred admitted. "Peanuts and dirt."

Soon the grubs lay in a pinkish, writhing pyramid. Fred tried to feel grateful that they had any food at all. He failed, badly.

Lila picked the three plumpest and offered them, palm up, to Max.

"No! That's not food. Max only eats actual food. Mama says don't eat insects."

Lila sighed. "He talks about himself as if he were another person when he's nervous."

"Max isn't nervous," said Max. "Maxie is just being good." He began to hiccup. "I want to go home," he said.

"I know you do," said Lila. She pulled him closer. "But this is all we have. I don't know what else to do, Maxie."

He pushed her away. "Mama would know!" His nail caught on the cut on Lila's cheek.

"But Mama's not here!" She blinked hard and wiped her nose on her wrist.

"What if we fried them?" said Fred. "And made them into a pancake?"

"Fry on what? We haven't got a pan," said Con.

"But we've got stones," said Lila. She scrubbed her face with her top and tried to sound bright. "We could make chocolate pancakes. Sort of."

"Sort of," said Con. "Really quite amazingly *sort of.*"

Fire

THE GRUBS, WHEN MIXED WITH THE COCOA beans and pounded with a clean stick, turned into a paste, which, if you squinted and were of an optimistic temperament, looked like flour and water.

"Now we just make a fire and cook them," said Fred.

"Just," said Con.

"We need flint," said Fred.

"And bits of kindling," said Lila.

"And *matches*," said Con.

"I'll do the kindling," said Fred. Most of the wood surrounding them had dried since the rain the night before. He held the hem of his shirt in his teeth and made a hammock for the wood. The night in the jungle had not improved the taste of the cloth. He tipped the wood into a pile a few paces away from the den.

"There were flints in there," said Lila. "We could rub away the moss and use them to make a spark. Flints don't go off."

"Flint isn't enough by itself," said Fred. "I've tried. You need a bit of steel."

Lila ducked into the den to fetch the flint. Con was staring at Fred's watch. "What's that made of?"

Fred stared down at the watch, covering it protectively with his hand. "Glass. And steel," he said. "My father gave it to me, when I went to boarding school."

"But it's broken," said Con.

"I know that," he said.

"So," said Con. "If it's broken, it's not really a watch anymore, is it? But what it *is*, is a lump of steel."

Fred jerked his hand back. His father never bought him birthday gifts; he had left his secretary to take Fred to Harrods to pick out something sensible. This was the only gift Fred could remember his father choosing himself. He had had it engraved with Fred's initials.

Lila smiled. Her voice had sympathy in it, but grit, too. "It might be the only way," she said.

THE EXPLORER · 51

"Fine!" said Fred. He had an unaccountable, absurd need to cry. "Fine! We'll use it."

"Can I have first try?" asked Con.

"It's my watch!"

"I know. But I've never lit a fire before," she said, "not even the ones in the fireplaces at home. Not allowed." There was longing, and hunger, in her eyes. She looked away from him, turning the flints in her hands as if they were jewels. There was something written in her face, Fred thought, something in a code he couldn't begin to read.

"Here." Slowly, he undid the strap. He held the watch in his fist, surreptitiously tracing the letters on the back with his thumb. Con watched in silence. He put it in her palm. "I get second go."

Lila heaped shredded leaves and dried grass in a pile. "You do it over that," she said, "so the spark has something to catch."

Con struck the back of the watch against the stone. Fred winced. She overshot, and dug the flint into her own skin. She said nothing, tried again. She bit down on her tongue, concentrating, her eyebrows furrowed so deeply they nudged against her eyelashes.

Suddenly, flint and steel let off a tiny spark. Con was so stunned she fumbled the flint.

"Again!" shrieked Max. "Again, again!"

The spark came again, a brief flare into the world that vanished as it came.

"It needs to be lower over the kindling," said Lila.

Con struck again, and again and again until her fingers were bleeding; suddenly a spark caught against a blade of grass, which caught against another. Fred's heart leaped and he dropped to his stomach and blew on it, terrified he would blow it right out. The flame faltered.

"No! No, no, don't die!" said Con.

Lila added a handful of dry moss. Fred blew again. The fire seemed to breathe in, and then exhaled a cough of flames. Max whooped. Lila held out a sheaf of twigs. The fire caught at them, making five burning fingers, ate them whole. It belched upward.

"More!" said Max. He was dancing in a tight circle, slapping at his own ribs. "Feed it more!"

Fred added a handful of bone-dry leaves, and then another and another. The fire made a noise like an idea being born, a roar that sounded like hope, and sent up a column of flames.

They rocked back on their ankles, grinning at one another.

"We could sleep in shifts," said Con, "to make sure it doesn't go out." She looked at the fire with proprietorial pride. "We made that. By ourselves."

Fred quietly put the watch in his pocket. It was scratched now and deeply dented, but, out of sight, he clutched it so tightly it dug a circular bruise into his palm.

"It's the most beautiful fire I've ever seen," said Lila.

"Yes," said Con. "By far."

Max bit lightly at Lila's arm. "Can we eat now? I'm so hungry I might die."

Fred scrabbled in the dust with his nails until he found a flat stone, and balanced it, wobbling dangerously, on four green-wood sticks over the center of the flames. Lila divided the grub paste into four balls, and spread them on the stone.

Eventually the pancakes began to bubble. Lila poked them. "They're getting harder," she said.

"And they smell like a shoe," said Con. "That probably means they're done."

One of the trees near the den had vast fleshy leaves, as big as serving dishes. Fred pulled four of them down and dropped a grub pancake onto each one. They were hot to the touch, and gooey.

"They're probably best while they're so hot you can't taste them," said Fred. He bit off half the pancake, trying not to chew too much. It tasted disconcertingly animal. It was, he thought, like eating porridge mixed with fingernail grime, but it was better—wildly, infinitely better—than nothing.

Con nibbled the corner of hers. She grimaced, but she did not spit it out. "To be honest, it's not that much worse than school dinners," she said. And she smiled half a smile.

Max kept his food scrunched in his fist, guarding it from the others: "I don't like sharing," he said. His pancake oozed out from between his fingers, and he licked it off. "Yuck," he said. "Is there any more?"

The clearing was growing darker every minute. Con stood. "I'm going to go and use the"—she hesitated, and colored—"the . . . lavatory . . . so don't come over there. Or look around. Or I'll punch you." She paused. "Please."

"We could decide on a place," said Fred. "And dig some holes."

"Yes!" said Lila. "And we could stake out a path—and

then nobody would get lost if they had to go in the night."

They got up, all four of them standing close together in the gathering dark, and began looking for a suitably large tree, far enough from their fire, but not far enough away to risk getting lost.

"This one's big," said Fred.

"And this one," said Con. The trees were immense, stretching at least as high as a church.

"We could make that one the boys' toilet, and this one the girls'," said Con.

Lila's smile was sudden, and enormous; it showed that one of her teeth was wonky, and she had a dimple in her cheek. "We could call it the lavo-tree."

It wasn't terribly funny, but once Fred started laughing he couldn't stop. Con choked and had to bite her fist. Max's laughter sent a ribbon of snot flying out across the glade. They laughed loudly enough to scare the birds, and to make the distant monkeys roar angrily from their night perches in the trees around them.

The Raft

I T WAS FRED'S IDEA TO BUILD A RAFT. HE KNEW that it wasn't, by any stretch of the imagination, what Con would call a reasonable risk, but following the river was the only way he could think of to get home. The river moved fast, and the splash and spit and spray of it sounded like a summons through the jungle.

"A raft?" said Lila. "From what?"

They were sitting in the clearing in the morning sun, clammy with sleep and dew. They'd slept inside the den, taking shifts to watch the fire. It had not been a good night. It had grown cold, and Max's feet, which had begun the night in their proper place, had ended up in Fred's left ear. Fred's brain had chewed up the fears he had pushed aside during the day and spat them back at him while he slept. He'd woken, screaming, at dawn.

"We'll make it from wood," said Fred. He swept some

of the dew from the grass around him and rubbed his face with it. "There's a lot of wood available."

"Do you know how?"

"I've read a lot of books about it," he said. In the books, explorers cascaded down rivers, shouting things like "Tally ho!"; but he assumed that was not compulsory. And Fred had read in an article on the front page of the *Times* about one man, Christopher Maclaren, who had lived for months on a raft, eating fish and drinking river water. He had made it sound easy.

"Why do we need a raft?" said Con.

"It would get us out of here."

"To England?" she asked.

"To Manaus, and there would be people there who will get us home."

"On a raft? To Manaus?" said Con. Her voice was thick with disbelief.

"People crossed the Atlantic Ocean on rafts," said Fred.

"They were *adults*."

"There's nothing that says only adults can make rafts," said Fred, exasperated. "You don't need a license."

"Fred's right: We should try," said Lila. "I think it's a good idea."

"I knew you'd say that!" said Con. "I knew you'd agree with him!"

"But"—Lila looked bewildered—"don't you want to go home? Don't you want to see your mama?"

"Of course I do!" Con spat.

Fred looked down at the floor. He had heard Con crying in the night, calling for help in her sleep.

"But if we just wait here," said Lila, "we'll wait until we die!"

"People will be looking for us! We should just stay here, and they'll come," said Con.

Lila shook her head. "The jungle is very big, and we're small."

"I'm not," said Max promptly.

"You're small compared to a thousand miles of rain forest, Max."

"We can send up smoke signals," said Con. "We already have some fire; let's use it!"

"We'd have to burn down half the jungle to make one big enough to reach that high," said Lila.

"And a fire that big would kill us instead of getting us rescued," added Fred.

Con was going red. "I don't want to, all right? I really, really don't want to get on a raft and risk my life because someone else thinks it's a good idea!"

"It might not be a good idea," said Lila, "but it's the only one we've got!"

Fred's skin was beginning to ache, and his stomache to clench; it always did when people argued. He stood up.

"I'm going to make a raft. You don't have to help if you don't want to."

The raft took more time, and involved more blisters, than Fred had expected. But it quieted the roar of fear behind his ribs, to be doing something.

"It's not going to work," said Con. Her arms were crossed so tightly across her chest that her fingers were almost touching at the back. "And we shouldn't make ourselves hungry and tired when the only food we have is grubs."

Fred said nothing, and went on pulling immense branches down from the trees. Most were too firmly attached to be any good, but he had found that if he put his whole weight on them and swung his legs, every now and then one would break off with a satisfying crack. He worked faster and faster, brushing away leaves and insects as they fell in his eyes.

Once the wood was piled in a heap, Lila heaved each piece to the fire. She laid each one across the flames. When the middle burned away, they were left with two pieces of roughly equal length, each as long as she was tall.

"I'll take off the burnt bits," she said. "It might as well look neat." She hacked away the burnt edges with a flint, getting steadily more covered in soot.

"I want to help!" said Max. He strode around the clearing with his chest out, tugging liana vines down to the ground and piling them up. "I'm actually the best at helping," he said. He sat down and began to make the vines talk to one another.

After a few hours Con unwound herself from her angry ball of limbs. Silently, she approached Max. She took up one of his vines, and a flint, and began to skin back the rough bark on the liana to expose the softer core, thick as a rope and almost as supple. She covered her face with her hair as she worked, and she refused to meet anybody's gaze.

Fred watched her from the corner of his eye. Con was different when she worked. Before, she had seemed all elbows and claws, touch-me-not and defensive eyebrows. But now she seemed absorbed, barely breathing as she bent over the vines.

Fred had never been as proud of anything as he was of that raft. It distracted him from the pounding hunger in his stomach and head. He hauled the branches to the water's edge, dragging them one in each hand, back and forth, beating out a path between the river and their clearing.

Con held out a handful of liana vines. "Here," she said. "For rope. Maybe. I don't know."

"We could dip them in the water to soften them," suggested Lila.

"Thank you," said Fred. "They'll be perfect for tying corners."

Con nodded, unsmiling.

Fred soaked the lianas, and wound them round and round his fist until they were supple. His hands prickled with splinters and he bit them out with his teeth. He sweated so much that his shirt turned into a sort of wearable pond.

For lunch they ate the cocoa beans, raw. They were not delicious.

"It feels like an insult to chocolate to eat them," said Con.

To try to fill their stomachs, they chewed on the

white flesh that lined the pods, which tasted exactly like the eraser at the end of a pencil.

"This isn't food," said Max. His chin and lip were quivering.

"You have to eat it, Max," said Lila. "There's nothing else."

"It tastes mean." Max dug his fist into his eye. "I want to go home!"

"I know," said Fred. "Me too." He decided he couldn't face any more grubs that day, and set aside the last of the cocoa-plant larvae. He turned back to the chunk of wood he was hacking in two with a jagged-edged stone. "We're trying."

As the sun set, Lila and Fred and Con went foraging, dragging a wailing Max behind them. Con found purple berries growing in great cascades on a tree.

"They're *açaí* berries!" said Lila. "People eat them at home. Or"—she frowned, looking down at the pile—"maybe you're supposed to make them into tea?"

Fred tried one. "It tastes a bit like a blackberry," he said, "if the blackberry were angry with you." But it was a relief to have something to chew.

Con tried one and sighed. "I miss school dinners," she said.

"They might be better roasted?" said Lila.

They were not better roasted, but they ate them anyway. Fred crouched by the fire and crammed handfuls into his mouth, trying desperately to fill the churning hole where his stomach was usually located.

That night he woke in sudden and excruciating need of the lavo-tree. Con, watching the fire, grinned as he sprinted past. Minutes later Lila woke with the same trouble, followed by Con and a hopping, wailing Max.

It was not, all in all, an easy night. Fred waded through his dreams until morning and woke feeling like he'd been kicked in the stomach. He turned on his side, groaning, and glimpsed though a hole in the green wall of the den the pile of vines they had prepared the day before. He sat bolt upright. *The raft!* he thought. He should be able to finish it that day.

The others were asleep, sprawled on their stomachs in the warmth of the den. He scrambled out of the shelter and ran down to the river where he had stacked the wood. The sun was hot and the air was clear; already, his skin had burned a furious red, but he barely felt it as he knelt by the pile of branches.

He looped each of the branches together with lianas,

working a figure eight, tying them so many times over that the raft was deep green, every inch embroidered with vines. Fred worked fast, biting down on his wrist and swearing as quietly as he could when he drove a thorn into his thumb.

He made four squares, each about six feet by six feet. Then he stacked them into two thicker squares, and tied the two squares together, tugging the knots with his teeth.

"Yuck." He spat out a beetle that had been on the vine. Then he stood back. The raft was rough edged and stained with soot, but it was sturdy, a double-thick, twelve-by-six-foot slab of wood.

Fred dragged it down to the very edge of the water, drops of sweat running down his nose and into his mouth. He wished, wildly, that he could take a photograph; he could almost see how his father would raise his eyebrows in surprise and pleasure. Reluctantly, he turned back to the clearing.

Maiden Voyage

LILA WAS WAITING OUTSIDE THE DEN. HER arms were wrapped around her knees, and she was glaring at him furiously. "You! I thought you were dead!"

"I was down by the river."

"Scratch a message in the dirt next time!"

"Yes, sorry." But Fred could barely concentrate on what she was saying. "The raft is ready! Will you come and try it out?"

"Max has to brush his teeth first. His breath is disgusting. It's scaring the dragonflies."

Lila picked four twigs and shredded the tops with her fingernails until they looked like paint brushes.

"Here." Lila handed one to Fred. "If our teeth drop out, it will just make everything worse."

It did feel better, Fred had to admit, to sweep some

of the fuzz from his teeth. But he was bursting with impatience. He gave three scrubs and dropped the brush.

"Come on!" he said, as soon as Con had spat, decorously, into the stagnant puddle.

Fred led them at a run down to the river. They stood panting while he showed them where the loops had been made double thick, and how he had added extra branches all the way around the outside.

"What do you want us to do," said Con, "clap?"

Fred did, secretly, just a little, but he grinned. "No. I want you to get on it."

He edged the raft onto the bank. It slid down the mud, landed on the water with a splash, tipped up on its right side—Fred drew in his breath—and righted itself. It swayed on the water, steady as a battleship; it was more beautiful, Fred thought, than any millionaire's yacht. He kept a firm hold of the liana tied to the right-hand corner.

"It floats!" said Max.

"Of course it floats," said Con. "It's wood."

Fred waded into the water, crossed his fingers, and hauled himself up. The raft dipped and spun under his weight as he climbed on, then steadied, rocking on the current. He paddled with his hands closer to the bank.

"Climb on!" he said.

"Max, wait—," said Lila.

Before anyone could stop him, Max had tipped himself headfirst down the bank into the river. He came up spitting mud. "Pull me up!" he said.

Fred hefted him by his armpits. Con and Lila followed more slowly, studying the water for piranha. Fred offered a hand to each. Lila took it; Con did not. The raft shook as they arranged themselves, but soon they were sitting, crouched on the wood and vines, bobbing high on the water.

"It works!" said Max.

"For now," said Con ominously.

"Let's go downriver!" said Fred.

"Why?" demanded Con. "We know it floats with us on it. That's what you wanted."

"We needn't go far. Just to test it?"

Here, under the cover of the trees, the current was slow, but out in the middle of the river, it spat and bubbled with speed. Fred could feel his skin twitching to send the raft down those waters.

"Let's try," said Lila. Her knuckles were pale where she was gripping the edge of the raft, but her eyes were hungry with curiosity. "If we're going to sail it to Manaus, we need to test it first."

Fred seized the pole he had made; he had smoothed it with the edge of a flint, and it was twice as tall as he was. The raft bucked under them. Fred felt his heart buck in unison.

"Careful!" said Con. The skin around her nose and lips was grayish green. "Don't go too fast. We need to be able to get back."

But the current caught at the raft and spun them, dragging at the wood and pushing it fast downriver. They sank a little in the water but remained upright. Fred ducked as an overhanging branch threatened to hit him in the eye.

"Is that a caiman?" asked Con, pointing at the far shore.

Max's eyes widened. "Make it go away!"

"No! Of course not. Con's being silly, it's just a log," said Lila, taking her brother's wrist in her hand. But, over his head, she met Con's eyes and whispered, "Maybe." Fred steered closer to the bank, his heart thumping.

They sped down the corridor of green. Fred tried to hold their course with the pole. Green trees dipped into the water on either side of them, like curtains at the theater, Fred thought, with the river as the stage. Two bright birds with yellow bellies flapped overhead.

"Blue macaws!" said Lila. "I tried so hard to persuade Mama to let me have one of those as a pet, but she said Max was loud enough on his own, without a parrot."

"It's funny," said Con. "I never really thought much about birds before. The birds here make the birds in England look like they're dressed for a job interview."

The sun beat down on the river, sending up green and silver light into their eyes. Fred followed the current, down the stream. They came to a fork in the river. "Someone will have to remember which way we've come," he said, "or we'll get lost."

There was a pause. Then Con said, "I'll remember, if you like."

Fred looked around, surprised. Con hadn't struck him as the volunteering sort.

"I've got—I've got a photographic memory, actually," she said.

"Really?" asked Lila, fascinated. "You mean, you see pictures? Do you remember everything that way, or only some things?"

"Mostly just maps, and formulae, and blueprints for things. I used to like taking them out to look at, at lunch break, in school. In my head, I mean. The others thought I was weird."

"In that case they're stupid," said Lila bluntly. "I'd love to be able to do that."

The raft swept round a corner with Fred poling hard.

"We turned left coming out, so the final turn home will be right," said Lila.

"Right: right," said Con. She grinned. Her smile changed the whole shape of her face: Her cheeks rose and pushed her eyes into little squints, and her mouth stretched up and out to her earlobes. Her touch-me-not look vanished. "If you shout out the directions, we could do it together. If you want."

Fred kept poling. The branch was giving him blisters on the pads of his hands, but he didn't slow. There was a twist, he found, that he could give the pole that made them move faster. It blew Max's snot in a high ribbon up his face. The sun was hot and sharp out here. The air tasted brand new.

"Faster!" shouted Max. He rocked backward and forward on his haunches.

They hadn't gone far before there was another fork; one looked choked with weeds, so Fred chose the other. "Left!" called Lila.

"Left," echoed Con, and nodded.

The left bend took them into a thinner river, winding slowly among close-set trees. Fred pulled up his pole and they drifted, staring down into the water. A shoal of fish swam, helter-skelter, under the raft. Max leaned dangerously over the edge, dangling his fingers in the water.

Suddenly, Con jumped. The hair on her arms rose up in a blond wave. "What's that?"

"What's what?"

"Something down there. Silver. Down there! A piranha!" Con's voice came out thin and high. "Max, get your hands out of the water!"

They all peered down into the water. There was something small and silver, trapped among the weeds. "It's not moving," said Fred.

"What is it?" said Con.

"It's . . . I think it's not alive," said Lila.

"A dead piranha?" said Con.

"It's . . . a silver box?" said Lila. "It's hard to tell. It's probably just a trick of the light?"

"I'm going to jump in and see," said Fred. "Just quickly."

"No, you're not!" said Con.

Lila, very softly, took hold of his wrist. "Don't," she whispered. "It wouldn't be clever."

"But it could be a knife!" said Fred. "It looks man-made. Please. You keep the raft close by. I need to see. I'll be in and out: It's simple."

"Fred!" said Con.

He pulled off his shirt, evaded Max, who tried to grab his ankle, and jumped over the edge of the raft.

The water was smooth here, without the current, and cool against his skin. Fred kicked downward. Weeds wrapped themselves around his ankles as he went deeper. His lungs began shrieking at him. The silver something was just a little farther—he brushed it with his fingertips, kicked one final kick, and snatched it. It was sharp against his fingers.

He shot to the surface. "Got it!" He held his fist up to show them, treading water.

But the two girls weren't looking at him. They were staring into the water a few feet from the raft.

"What's that?" whispered Lila.

Fred glanced down. There was something black undulating through the water toward him.

Fred gasped, swallowed a mouthful of water, and began to choke.

"An eel!" said Max brightly.

"An electric eel!" said Lila.

"Swim!" screamed Con. She snatched the pole and tried to steer toward Fred, jabbing the branch feverishly into the water. Lila held out her hand, over the edge of the raft.

Fred swam the distance to the raft faster than he had ever moved in his life. He launched himself onto the wood. The raft tipped drunkenly under his weight. Con threw herself to the opposite end to stop it overturning, and Lila's hands grabbed at him, small but surprisingly strong, hauling him up.

Fred lay on his stomach, gasping for breath, staring into the water.

The eel was immense. It looked like a deep-gray snake, as long as a grown man, winding in and out of the weeds.

Lila sucked in breath, and some of her own hair. "Oh, wow," she breathed. It wasn't just fear in her voice; it was fascination, too.

"Are eels dangerous?" asked Con.

"I don't know—but if you call someone an eel—," gasped Fred, coughing. His heart was trying to break out from his chest. He swallowed. "It's not a compliment. So maybe."

"They are. Very," said Lila. "They pass an electric

current through the water to shock their prey, and then eat them. They probably wouldn't be able to kill something Fred's size, but for Max it would be different." She was shaking. She picked up the pole and, very slowly, so as not to risk tipping them all in, began to guide them away—away from the eel, and away from the canopy of trees.

"What was it, down there?" asked Con.

"Here." Fred opened his fist. It was a rusty rectangle, made of tin, colored silver with blue swirly writing.

"It's an empty sardine tin!" said Con, her voice full of disgusted disappointment. "That's all."

"Yes," said Fred. He rubbed at the rust on the tin, and closed his fingers tightly around its jagged edge. A sardine tin in the wildest place in the world. "That's all."

Sardines

I T TOOK LONGER TO COAX THE RAFT BACK upstream; Lila steered them close to the bank, and they hauled their way along on overhanging branches when the pole wasn't enough. The branches hung low, and all four were covered in ants and spiderwebs by the time they reached their home stretch of river, with fresh scratches on their hands.

"It was here," said Con. "I recognize the way those vines wrapped around that branch."

The branch stuck out conveniently over the river. It was perfectly placed to act as a mooring branch; it jutted out at the ideal angle, right above a bank of black Amazon soil.

Fred stood, wobbling hard, on the raft.

"Watch it!" said Con.

The branch was just over his head; it was covered in

tendrils where it met the tree, and shone green in the sunlight. He grabbed hold of it, tied a loop in the end of his liana rope, and hung it over the branch.

"That's perfect!" said Lila. "Like a coat hook for our boat."

"It *is* perfect." Fred stayed standing, looking up at the branch in his hand. He peered closer. "It's perfect because someone made it perfect."

There was a beat of silence.

Then: "What do you mean?" asked Con. She spoke very quietly.

Fred didn't answer. He moved the branch to and fro under its covering of vines. It creaked backward and forward under his hand. The vines wound like a rope around the branch in a figure eight, repeated over and over.

"It didn't grow here. It's been tied on."

Max was staring openmouthed. "Who did it? Did you?"

"No, Maxie," said Lila quietly. "Not him. Somebody else."

Fred looked behind him. A gust of wind caught a pile of fallen leaves and spun them across the forest floor. The back of his neck prickled.

He reminded himself again that trees do not keep secrets.

They walked back to the clearing in single file. Fred came last. He turned to look backward at every step. The rustling in the bushes seemed to follow them; but it was just the wind, he told himself.

Wind is a trickster. It plays havoc with your courage.

The fire still had hot embers at its heart, and Fred lay down on his stomach in the grass and earth, blowing at it like a bellows, his chin inches from the fire. His eyes were red and smoky by the time it was rekindled, but the roar of it sent a wave of relief through his chest. The fire was the closest thing they had to a weapon, and its warmth felt like safety.

Lila was arranging their shoes, which had been soaked on the raft, in a circle around the ashes. "Can I see the thing you found in the water?" she asked.

Fred held it out. Most of the writing was covered in rust, but he could see, written on its base, the ingredients. "Look at the bottom," he said. "It says, 'Canned in Plymouth.'"

Lila looked blank.

"Plymouth is in England," said Fred. "Down by the sea."

"I didn't know you had fish in England!" said Max.

"Of course we have fish; what do you think we eat?" said Con.

"Crumpets," said Max. "And cigars."

"But if the tin comes from England—," began Lila.

"Then it must have come with whoever made the camp," said Fred. "An explorer, maybe."

"Who goes exploring with sardines?" asked Con.

"People used to come out here with all sorts of things. Pianos, and china ornaments. Sardines seem normal, in comparison," said Fred. He felt a hot surge rising in his chest. If the person who made the camp had been English, he might have been one of the explorers from the newspapers Fred had read, one of the explorers who never returned: Percy Fawcett, Simon Murphy, Christopher Maclaren.

"I had a book," said Fred, "about a man called Hiram Bingham. He was climbing and he came across a whole city, built by the Incas. It wasn't exactly dis-covering, because some of the Peruvians knew about it—but nobody else did. Can you imagine? It would be like suddenly finding the ruins of Birmingham in a thousand years' time."

Lila moved closer. Her eyes were set far apart in her face, eyes that could look full of many different things at once. Now they radiated curiosity. "I've heard about it—it's called Machu Picchu."

"Yes! That was the name. Usually, though, the men just go missing."

"Like us?" said Max.

"Sort of," said Fred. "Except usually it's because they're dead. Which we're not."

"*Yet,*" said Con ominously.

Fred ignored that. "And there was this man called Percy Fawcett—he was looking for a ruined city. He called it the City of Z. And then not that long ago—it was in 1925, I think—he just disappeared. And another man, Christopher Maclaren, he went on an expedition to find out if Fawcett's dream was real. He was my favorite; he wrote letters about waking up to find maggots growing in the crook of his elbow."

"How lovely," said Con. "Did the maggots get him?"

"Nobody knows. He sent a telegram, and then he disappeared." Fred hesitated. "I memorized it, actually."

"How does it go?" asked Lila.

Fred cleared his throat. "'Just a line from this last outpost of civilization to advise you that I am about to go out of communication. I am well and fit, and there is every hope of a successful issue to the expedition, risky as it is in some ways.'"

Con raised both eyebrows. "He sounds fun."

"Newspapers want people to sound like that. As if they have very clean shoes. But I know he wasn't like that. The other men said he was the maddest and bravest of a mad, brave generation."

"Why did you memorize it, though?"

Fred blew on the fire again, so they wouldn't see his face reddening. "I just liked the idea that there's still things that we don't know. At school it's the same thing, every day. I liked that it might be all right to believe in large, mad, wild things."

The journey on the raft had taken up the whole morning, but still the afternoon stretched ahead of them, thick and green and vibrating with heat.

"We need more wood," said Fred. They would burn through what they had by the time dark came. They needed so many things, he thought: food, and a plan or a map or a passing ship—but at least wood was something he knew where to find.

His vision swam as he stood; he was growing weaker, and the blood in his veins felt thinner.

At first Fred went fast, his head down, marking the trees with an X scratched in the bark, watching his feet among the roots and fallen branches.

But soon he began to slow. There was so much to look at: so much that was strange, so much that was new and vast and so very palpably alive.

The trees dipped down their branches, laden with leaves broad enough to sew into trousers. He passed a tree with a vast termite nest, as big as a bathtub, growing around it. He gave it a wide berth.

The greenness, which had seemed such a forbidding wall of color, was not, up close, green at all, Fred thought. It was a thousand different colors: lime and emerald and moss and jade and a deep, dark, almost black green that made him think of sunken ships.

Fred breathed in the smell. He'd been wrong to think it was thick, he thought; it was detailed. It was a tapestry of air.

The trees clustered more closely together the

farther he walked. The light grew dimmer, though he was sure it was still midafternoon: a deep green filtering down through a roof of leaves and vines. He heard something move in one of the great green bushes that clustered around his feet.

"Hello?" he called. He stepped backward. "Hi?"

As he called, something sharp scraped against his arm.

He jumped, and leaped away, and felt his mouth fill with the taste of fear: bile and tin. But it wasn't a snake, or even a spider.

"Being stupid," muttered Fred. It was just a bush.

Or, perhaps it wasn't even a bush. He leaned closer. It was a clump of spiky fruit.

"A pineapple," he whispered aloud.

Fred felt his fingertips prickle, shot through with the spark of discovery. This, he thought, must be what Columbus had felt like.

He reached out to pull the fruit from its throne of leaves—and then snatched his hand back, watching blood swell from a serrated gash in his thumb. "Ach," he whispered.

He braced himself, wrenched up five of the biggest pineapples, and set off at a run; a slightly jolting run, checking every few trees for the *X* and doubling back three times. At last he burst through the trees at the edge of the clearing.

He was met by a scream. "Get back!"

Lila was standing in front of Max, one arm pushing him behind her, a stick pointed in the direction of Fred's throat. Con stood behind her, fists raised.

"I brought some pineapple!" panted Fred. Then he took in the scene. He grinned. "Were you planning to kill me?"

"We thought you were a wild animal," Con said, flushing deep red. "Call out, next time you come charging straight at us!"

It was Max who saw the pineapple in his arms. He gave a roar of joy that shook the fire and sat down, his bared teeth ready. He held out both hands. "Mine mine mine!" he said.

Fred turned the pineapples in his hands, looking for a way in. Gingerly, he bit into the side of the fruit. A spike jabbed up his nose, and another dug into his gum, but the juice was the most spectacular thing he had ever tasted. It was sweet and warm and it sparked on his tongue.

"It's amazing!" he said. "It's like eating electricity."

Con took a bite of hers. "It's more like waging a war than seems fair, for dessert," she said.

Fred used his nails to scrape away the skin, and dug out a handful of flesh. He held it out to Max. "Here. You'll like it."

Lila was bent over her fruit, her hair hanging over her lap. Now she looked up, and grinned. "Are you sure you wouldn't like a flint?" she said. She'd cut into her pineapple with one of the arrowhead flints and carved out rough palm-size chunks. She laid them out in a row.

"Oh. That might be an improvement," said Fred. Somehow, he had pineapple juice in his ear. Con laughed.

Lila hacked the fifth pineapple into quarters. "For breakfast," she said. She wrapped each piece in a large leaf and stacked them outside the den.

Abacaxi

THE NEXT MORNING FRED STARTLED AWAKE with a handful of grass and moss in each hand. The nightmares were getting worse. He blinked, looking around. He was not in the den, but lying in the clearing near the pool. He had dreamed he had heard his father weeping, which was ridiculous; his father had never cried in his life. He had dreamed he was running home. Deep asleep, he must have heaved his body across the clearing. There were patches torn out of the grass around him.

He brushed the mud from his face, and crawled over to the den. Lila and Con lay asleep, their hair tangled together. But the pineapple wasn't there. Nor was Max.

It took a moment to be sure he wasn't still asleep. Then he jumped to his feet, whispering, "Please, no. No, no, no."

But there were no bones, no blood. Surely a jaguar would have left bones?

Fred shook Lila awake. "Max is missing!"

"Whatyouwant?" she muttered. She tucked her knees up to her chin and batted him away. "M'sleeping."

"Max isn't here!"

"What?" Lila sat bolt upright. Her eyes still had sleep in the corners, and they were wild.

"Max?" she called. She jumped to her feet, scrambling out of the den, tearing her skin on the thorns. "Max!" She stared around the clearing. Her voice rose to a roar. "Maxie! Where are you?"

Con jolted awake and came barreling out of the den. "What's happening? Are you all right?" She took one look at Lila's stricken face. "Max!" she called. "Stupid idiot boy! What if something's eaten—"

"Don't!" said Lila, rounding on her. "Don't you dare!" And then, louder, her voice scraping at the air, "Max! MAX!"

"He might be by the river?" said Fred.

"We'll split up," said Lila. "If I go down to the river, will you go back toward the plane?" She stumbled forward, dizzy with panic. "Max!"

One of the trees giggled.

Max stepped out from behind a cedar at the edge of the clearing. "Boo!" he said. He waggled his arms and legs and tongue at them. "I've been awake for hours! I'm bored."

"Max!" Lila's eyes were brick hard and ferocious. "You vile little brat! If you ever do that again, I'll tell Papa when we get home and he'll beat you with his shoe."

Max's face fell. "He wouldn't! He never hits me!"

"He would if I told him what you did!" She looked closer at him, her eyes narrowing. "Where did you go?"

"Secret!"

"And did you eat the pineapple?"

"Secret," said Max. He wiped guiltily at his cheek.

"Max!" Lila balled her fists. "Max, if you ate all our food, I don't care what Mama would say, I'll smack you so hard—"

Max pressed his lips together and shook his head. "Pick me up, Lila," he said.

"Tell us, Max! Where did you go?"

"Up!" His eyes welled up. "I'll tell you if you pick me up!" He began to shudder with huge, body-shaking sobs.

Lila gave a hiss of fury. She picked him up. The sobs ceased immediately.

"You can't get your own way just by crying!" said Con, her face tight with disgust.

He smiled up at her. His eyes were clear of tears. "Yes, I can," he said.

"Now tell me." Lila took hold of Max's chin. "Where did you go? Where's the pineapple? Did you steal it? Did you eat it all?"

"No! I wanted to share some with the animal."

"Which animal?"

"The monkey thing."

"Where?"

"By the lavo-trees," said Max. He was pouting. "I didn't do anything wrong. He was hungry. I was being kind."

Lila dropped Max on the ground. He gave a wail, but saw her face and stopped.

"Show me," said Lila. "Or I won't believe you."

An unexpected excitement gripped Fred. Lila began to run, the other three following, down the path they had hacked, toward the cluster of trees surrounding the immense trunk of the boys' lavo-tree.

Max was tugged along by the hand, his legs pounding double time to keep up. "Slow down!" he wailed. They passed the lavo-tree and moved out of the sunlight, into the thick-growing trees.

Suddenly, Max stopped. "It's there!" he pointed up at a low-hanging branch. "See! I *wasn't* lying!"

Above their heads rose a great flowering white tree. From one of the branches hung a small animal, unlike anything Fred had ever seen before. It was looking up with enormous eyes at a vulture in the branches above its head.

On the ground below it were three chunks of pineapple, untouched. And some distance away, two more vultures crouched over the corpse of a larger version of the same animal.

"Get away!" yelled Lila. She ran forward, kicking at the birds. "Get away from it!"

The two vultures on the ground took off, startled, but the vulture in the tree only ruffled its feathers. It was enormous, broad as a Labrador around the middle, and its eyes watched the tiny animal hungrily.

The animal on the branch let out a mew like a cat. It was gray brown with a cream face, a doglike snout, and immense black eyes. Its arms were long and chicken-bone thin, ending in curved claws. It was small enough to cup in your hands.

Lila ran to the base of the tree, gripped the lowest branch, and scrabbled with her feet against the trunk.

The vulture, feeling the tree shake, flapped its wings, cawed, and disappeared. Lila hauled herself into the branches. Her knees were shaking. Her breath was unusually loud.

She sat on the branch on which the animal perched and began to scoot forward, both hands gripping the branch. With quivering hands, she unwound its legs from the branch and rewound them around her own arm. The creature let out a mewling sound.

Lila began to edge backward along the branch. Fred could hear her whispering prayers under her breath.

She stumbled as she landed on the ground, and half fell, but made sure to keep the arm with the animal high above her head.

Max ran to her. "What is it? Let me see!"

"It's a sloth," said Lila. Her voice was low. "A baby sloth."

Fred stepped closer. It was one of the most extraordinary things he had ever seen. It was very ugly and very beautiful, both, at once. Its fur still had the fluffiness of babyhood.

"Let's make it play!" said Max. He grabbed at Lila's arm.

"No!" Lila seized his wrist, cradling the sloth against her chest. "Don't! You'll hurt it!"

The brother and sister glared at each other. "No, I won't! I'll be soft."

"Maxie, you mustn't. It's terrified; it doesn't have a mother to protect it. See, it's shaking."

"But I *love* it!" Max looked dangerously close to tears.

"But it doesn't need you to love it to death. It needs us to be slow," whispered Lila. "Come on, Maxie—let's take it back to the camp. You can bring the pineapple."

Back in the clearing, Lila made a bed of soft grass for the sloth. She set it down on its stomach, where it lay quivering, and held out the pineapple to it.

"I want to touch it!" said Max.

"No," said Lila, as she sat down. "Let him catch his breath."

The sloth shook. Lila shook. Every part of her radiated longing. It was probably best, Fred imagined, to leave people alone at such moments. People suddenly bludgeoned by passions are unpredictable. They might bite, or cry. He stepped backward, giving her room.

The sloth moved, very slowly, out of its bed and

toward Lila. It reached her shoe and crawled—so slowly Fred was sure he could hear its muscles stretching and retracting under its fur—into Lila's lap. With a peculiar, jerky grace, the sloth reached out and grasped the pineapple between its front claws.

Lila didn't seem to be breathing. But it was as if a light came out of her; she seemed to glow out into the forest.

The sloth struggled to arrange the fruit so it could bite it, but Lila didn't move. She sat, stock-still, watching as it sprawled itself more comfortably across her lap. It moved like an unoiled rocking horse, Fred thought.

Lila looked up and saw them. "I've never seen one in real life," she whispered. "People always told me sloths are slow, and stupid. But I think they're only slow the way a ballet is slow." Very, very softly, she laid a finger on the sloth's chest. "I can feel his heart. It's fast. It's a different rhythm."

The sloth finished chewing at the pineapple. It crawled up Lila's arm and clung to her, up near her shoulder, resting its head just below her right ear. It made a little snorting noise, and Lila's hair ruffled.

"He needs a name," said Con.

"I've never named anything," said Lila, her neck twisted to look at the sloth. He was trying, very slowly, to eat her earlobe.

"You don't have pets?" asked Fred. It seemed strange, in a person who was so clearly designed to live alongside living things.

"I was never allowed one. I begged and begged, but Mama and Papa move a lot for their work, and they said it wouldn't be fair." Lila looked hard at the sloth. She narrowed her eyes. Her lips formed a word.

"What's his name?" asked Max. "You have to tell us! It can't be a secret!"

"Abacaxi," she said.

"Yes," said Max authoritatively. "That's good."

"Say it again?" said Con.

"Abacaxi. It's Portuguese for pineapple," said Lila. "Baca, for short."

The Monkeys and the Bees

JUNGLES, FRED FOUND, WERE FULL OF COR-
ners and crannies; they held secrets. But the
secrets emerged in the most unexpected ways.
They would never, he thought, have found the scrap
of paper that changed everything if it hadn't been for
the joint efforts of the monkeys and the ants and the
bees.

Max saw them first, later that afternoon. He had
been lying on his back, staring at the sky, while Lila
and Con and Fred sat by the fire and tried to make a
plan.

The problem was that despite being told very firmly
to stay put, Max kept trying to explore; and he was a
small five-year-old in a very large jungle.

"How sure are you," Lila asked Fred, "that the raft
will hold?"

Fred considered. The raft was wide, and strong, and the vines wrapped so thickly to secure it that the raft was more green than brown; it looked like a square of floating field. But, he thought, the pilot had presumably been just as certain about the plane.

"Medium sure." He saw Con's face. "High medium. And walking would take weeks," he said. "We know Manaus is on the Amazon—so if we sail downriver, we should reach it!"

Max approached, and sat on Lila's feet, tugging at her sock. "Lila!" He dug a chunk of snot from his nose and wiped it on the grass.

"Except we don't know if Manaus is upriver or downriver from here," said Con. "So we have a fifty percent chance of death."

"Lila!" said Max. "Listen to me!"

"But there's a fifty percent chance of life!" said Fred. Con smirked; he resisted the urge to flick Max's snot at her.

"Can you hear yourself?" she said. "Do you know how insane that sounds?"

"Lila!" Max tugged harder at her sock. "Did you see! Did you see how the monkeys fought the bees?"

"What do you mean?" asked Lila. Baca had taken up a

position draped across one of Lila's shoulders, back legs hooked under her armpit. He looked, Fred thought, like the epaulettes on his father's old army uniform.

"The monkeys won!" said Max. "I followed them!"

"Max! What are you talking about?" Lila picked him up and held his face close to hers, blazingly angry. "I thought you were in the den! You know you're not allowed to move! I *told* you! If I can't trust you, I'm going to tie you to me."

Max pouted. "I didn't go far! I stayed away because I don't like bees."

"Maxie, don't lie—there are no bees," said Lila. "I've seen every flying thing—ants and beetles and mosquitoes—but no bees."

"It was over there!" said Max. He pointed to the other side of the clearing, among tall rubber trees. "In the high bits."

Lila raised her eyebrows over Max's head. "Was this a dream, Max, or in real life?"

"Real life," said Max.

"I don't believe you."

"Real life!" Max looked furious. "Real life! The monkeys washed their hands in the ants and then they fought the bees."

"I have no idea what you're trying to describe," said Con, "but it sounds terrifying."

Max got up, roared, and stamped. He stepped on Con's knuckles. Con gave a yell and slapped at his ankles.

"That hurt!" she said.

"Don't hit him!" said Lila.

"You're not paying attention, any of you!" said Max. "Listen!"

Fred looked at Max; the boy's eyes were unhappy, and a little wild. "We *are* listening, Max," he said.

"No! Come!" Max took hold of Con's hand and pulled her up and into the trees, his small feet thumping determinedly into the earth.

Con looked surprised, but let herself be led, jogging beside him. She didn't comment on the state of Max's hand, which was sticky with unknown substances. Fred and Lila ran after them.

"There!" said Max. "They were there!"

He pointed up at an ants' nest, a great bulbous structure built on the tree's trunk, bulging out of it like a potbelly. There were no monkeys in sight.

"They were here really soon ago!" said Max. "They'll come back."

Skeptically, Fred sat down. Max sat on Lila's legs. Baca clung to Lila's shirt.

Sitting still and empty handed was not, Fred found, an easy thing to do. The things he was trying so hard not to think about—his father's face, his mother's voice—came crowding in. And darker things—all four of them starving, unfound, in the green clearing—crept toward him.

He tried to whistle, but his head swam, and he could only make a peculiar piping noise.

"Fred," whispered Lila, "you'll scare the monkeys."

And then, suddenly, the monkeys came. There were three of them, dark brown, strong limbed and sweet faced.

Fred watched in awe as they chased one another up and down the trees, chittering. They whirligigged around the trees, flicking their tails; and then the largest of the monkeys, a mother with a baby hanging from her neck, laid her paws on the ants' nest. The ants swarmed over the monkey's paws and up her arms, until her fur was black with them. Then, fast, before the ants could bite, the monkey rubbed her paws together.

Con touched Fred's sleeve. "Is she killing the ants?"

Fred watched the monkey lower her nose to her paws, and sniff, deeply. "Is it like a perfume? Or a sort of drug?" he asked.

Suddenly, all three monkeys, as if at a signal, turned and leaped away across the trees.

"Let's follow them!" said Lila.

It is not easy to keep pace with monkeys if you don't happen to be one yourself, and if you haven't eaten properly for days. They were all four weak, and Lila's hands were shaking. Con turned pale as they jogged after the monkeys' disappearing backs.

The monkeys leaped into the branches of the spreading rubber trees and halted.

"Bees!" said Max, in a profoundly self-satisfied voice. "I told you so!"

Far above their heads, so far it was blurred with distance, was a bees' hive. It was enormous, encased in a gray layer of resin, and the buzzing was astonishingly loud. Honey ran down the side of the tree.

Lila's eyes widened. She held Baca more tightly. "They don't attack sloths, do they?"

As they watched, the mother monkey approached the hive, broke open the protective layer, and plunged her paws into its depths. She broke off a piece of honeycomb and bit into it, dripping honey on her baby's head. The bees swarmed furiously but didn't go close enough to sting.

Lila's eyes were as wide as the sun. "I think the smell on her paws meant that the bees didn't attack," she said. "It must be a repellent."

"Let's try it!" said Fred, already on his feet.

"But what if it only works for monkeys?" said Con.

"Well, there's only one way to find out." He thought of dinner, which would be pineapples if there were any left, and cocoa grubs if there weren't. "Wouldn't you like some honey?"

"Just think, for a minute, before you—"

But Fred was already running. He wound his way back to the ants' nest, and waited, panting, for the others to catch up; then he laid his hands on its side. The ants swarmed onto his fingers and knuckles and wrists; it was like wearing a pair of black gloves.

"They tickle," he said.

"Now you rub your hands!" ordered Max. "Quick! *Quickly*, like the monkeys!"

A few of the ants swarmed up Fred's arms all the way to his chin, but they didn't seem disposed to bite. He rubbed his hands together, feeling a little guilty, and then sniffed. The smell was so strong that he gagged.

"You know when they put stuff on cuts at school?" he said. "It's like that."

"Disinfectant?" said Lila.

He rubbed his hands over his face, as he'd seen the monkey do, and up his arms. He gathered more ants and rubbed the smell onto his legs and ankles too, just in case.

Con pulled his hand down to her face so she could sniff. "It smells like ammonia!" she said. "Like my aunt's smelling salts!"

They ran back to the honey tree. Fred thought the others seemed to be giving him a wider berth than usual.

"You smell like a bad idea," said Max. "Like medicine."

At the foot of the tree, Fred looked up. The trunk was enormous; the bees were a distant cloud.

"Are you sure you don't want to stop to think for just one single second? To at least make a plan?" said Con.

"I'll be fine," said Fred. He had always loved climbing trees, the feeling of navigating an unknown land, upward.

The others watched him: Lila with expectant eyes, Con with one eyebrow and her upper lip raised, Max with his finger in his nose.

He seized a low branch and heaved himself up. Max cheered. Fred's legs scrabbled for purchase, and then found a knot in the bark and pushed upward.

He felt immediately that this was different; this was nothing like climbing at home. His muscles were weak, and less at his command; his arms and legs were bruised and had less pull and spring to them. It occurred to him with a jolt that he hadn't checked to see if the tree's wood was rotten. The tree creaked under him, loud as the hinge on a giant's gate.

"Damn," he whispered, very quietly.

He reached up for the next branch, and then the next, his shoes slipping and sliding on the smoothness of the bark.

"Oh, for goodness' sake," he heard Con say. "He's going to get himself killed."

"He'll be all right," said Lila. "Really."

"What if he's not, though? It'll be even harder stuck in this place with just three of us. Fred!" she called. "Please, just come down!"

Fred ignored her. He swung higher and faster. He set both feet on a thick branch, and looked above his head for a good handhold.

Suddenly, the branch under his feet snapped. His

legs flailed in the air, kicking against the trunk of the tree. He swung from his hands, feeling his fingers slip against the slick surface. He scrabbled with his right hand for another branch, his legs blindly seeking a foothold. His feet met solid wood again.

He tried to pull up to the next handhold, but his arms felt hollow, no more use than wool and straw. He stood on the branch, clutching the wood above his head, frozen. He tried not to think of what his father's face would look like if he heard his son had died climbing a tree.

"Look at him!" said Con below. "He's stuck."

"Are you all right?" called Lila.

"He's obviously not," said Con. "I'm not going to stand here and watch him die."

She stomped to the base of the tree, her shoulders hunched around her ears, and began to haul herself up, her jaw locked like a boxer's. She moved stiffly, but steadily, despite the shaking in her hands and knees.

Fred watched as she came to rest a few branches below him, staring up, hugging the trunk to her chest. Her ankles were wobbling with fear.

"What are you doing?" he asked through gritted teeth.

"Telling you to come down."

"No," said Fred. "I'm going up."

"Then I'm coming too."

"Why?"

"You look stuck."

"I'm not!" But it wasn't true, he knew; he had no feeling in his arms. He looked down at Con: Her face was bloodless, so white it was almost blue, but etched with determination. Flushing, he tried to arrange his expression into easy curiosity. "Even if I were, how would you be able to help?"

"I'll go ahead," she said, "and test the branches. If you have another scare like that, I'll bet you'd just fall and die."

"I wasn't scared," said Fred. The words were out of his mouth before he could stop them.

"Yes, you were," said Con, facing up the tree. "And so am I. So there."

She moved ahead. She went infinitely more slowly than he would have, and her face was set with an expression that looked like fury, but she climbed steadily, testing each branch with her feet and wiping her hands on her skirt at every move.

Fred unpeeled one hand from the branch. He

pushed back at the angry opera of fear. He followed Con.

Gradually, as Fred climbed, the sway and rhythm of it took over, and his breath returned to normal. The hive came into sight. There were hundreds, perhaps thousands, of buzzing insects.

"Bees don't have encouraging faces, do they?" said Con. Her voice was much higher than usual. "Do it quickly, so we can go down."

"Just a second." Fred crouched on the branch, his legs shaking a little, and stuffed leaves into his nostrils so the bees couldn't sting up his nose. "Don't come too close, or you'll get stung."

From far down below, he heard Lila call encouragingly, "You can do it!"

Max, unencouragingly, shouted, "But also, if you both fall, would you be angry if we ate you?"

Fred stood, wrapping one arm around a thick branch to the right of him. With the other, he reached up and left, out over the vast drop, and pushed his hand into the fist-size hole in the bees' nest that the monkey had made.

The buzzing grew louder and more furious. Fred braced himself. The bees swarmed angrily around him, and a few rebounded off his shorts, but not a single bee touched his skin. Triumphantly, Fred broke off a fistful of honeycomb, and then another.

"It works!" Fred said. A bee buzzed into his mouth; he swore and spat it out, jerking his head, and felt the tree sway under him.

"Where do we put it?" asked Con. She looked around, as if expecting a glass jar to be balanced in the crook of a branch.

"We could drop the chunks of honeycomb down to Lila," Fred said, "but they might get stuck in the branches."

"If all of this was for nothing—," Con began.

"No, I've got an idea."

He braced himself and looped one arm around a branch. With his free hand, he tucked his shirt into his shorts, then dropped the honey inside his shirt front. He licked his fingers.

"Agh!" he said. He had forgotten that they were covered in dust from the bark and the remnants of the ants, but even so the honey was spectacular. It made his skin buzz.

"Can I have some?" asked Con.

"I thought you wanted to get down."

She was shaking so hard her knees were jumping, but she lifted her chin defiantly. "If you can, I can."

It was as Fred edged around the great round trunk of the tree toward her that he saw it: something red, the size of an apple, tied tightly with vines to the branch.

His breath stopped. He leaned backward to see better.

"Fred!" screamed Con. "Don't!"

"I'm fine." He grabbed a handful of tree branch. "Look above your head."

The red thing was not a plant. It did not have the tinge of life to it.

"What is it?" She squinted upward. "The leaves are in the way!"

"I think it's leather."

"Like, a handbag?"

"No. Something else."

He edged around her, and upward. He unwound the thing from the tree as quickly as he could, his hands shaking. The branch he was on was broad, and he sat down on it, his legs hanging down on either side.

Con approached and sat, hugging the trunk with one shaking arm, facing him. "Don't open it now!" she said. "Wait until we're on the ground, you idiot!"

"Just quickly," said Fred. It was a red leather pouch, with a leather drawstring and the remnants of gold-embossed writing on the base. It was heavy. His hands were shaking as he opened it and pulled out a lump of metal.

"A tobacco tin," he said. It was rusty, but less rusty than the sardine tin.

"Let me see?" said Con. There were words on the side. She whispered them aloud, as if they were a spell. "Colliers Finest Tobacco. London Piccadilly."

"There's something else," he said. The tree rocked suddenly in the wind, and the thing slipped through his fingers. He caught it just in time; it was also rusty, and rough in his fingers. "A penknife!" he said.

"Is that everything?"

"I think so."

He brushed away a stray bee, and upturned the pouch over his palm. A piece of paper fell out.

"What's that?" said Con. "A letter?"

It was a sheet of paper from the blank end pages of a book, marked in ink and labeled with neat block capitals. In the corner there was a sketch of the points of a compass.

"It's a map," he said.

Goose bumps rose on his arms. Fred knew the power of maps. They gestured to hidden things. They were line drawings of the world's secrets.

He studied it. It was sketched in ink, which had faded in the creases of the paper. There were thin lines for tributaries, and a thick one for what he assumed must be the Amazon. In the far right-hand corner, there was an X. It had been scratched so fiercely the pen had pierced the paper.

"What do you think it's of? What's the X stand for?" Con's eyes were wide; she seemed to have forgotten they were fifty feet up in the sky.

"I don't know." Fred looked upward. The tree they sat in was taller than the others that surrounded it. Near the top, where it thinned to a spike, it stood high above most of the rest of the canopy. "I'm going farther up," he said. "If I can get above the canopy, I might be able to see."

"No, you're not! That would be insane—you're just showing off because you're embarrassed you got scared before."

Fred felt his ears grow red. "I'm going. Do you want to go back down or come with me?"

Con pulled down the corners of her mouth. "I'm coming too, obviously!"

They went slowly, testing each branch, as the branches got thinner and thinner. The branches became springy and fork-handle thin.

Suddenly Fred broke out from under a leafy branch and he found himself head and shoulders above the canopy. Below him, the river stretched purple and silver. Fred tried to keep his breathing steady. It was exactly as he had dreamed it, from his seat on the floor in a corner of the library.

"Look!" he said.

"I *am* looking!" said Con. She was just below him. Her eyes were screwed shut.

The river wound for miles around bends and swoops, disappearing into the horizon near the foot of a mountain. As he watched, a monkey skittered down from a tree and leaped away, curling its tail around branches as it swung past him.

"Open your eyes, Con!" said Fred. "You have to see!"

Con opened her eyes, and then opened them further, as wide as the sky. "I didn't know it would be like this! It's . . . bite-your-fist beautiful."

It looked, Fred thought, like someone had designed

it with a purpose in mind: someone who wanted the world to be as wild and green and alive as possible.

Very slowly, Fred let go of the tree with one hand. Fear rose up in his mouth but he reached into his pocket. He unfolded the paper.

It felt like a small, green miracle. The map matched exactly what he saw. It might almost have been drawn from precisely this position, or one very close.

He peered down at the map. "That's us," he whispered.

"And that bend, that's the place where we moored," said Con. There were ink curves, intricately sketched, that matched exactly—or almost exactly— the world below them.

"Where's the *X*?" asked Con.

Fred shielded his eyes. "That way. But I can't see anything." The horizon was a green smudge; he could not see where the river wound.

"We should mark where we are, on the map," said Con. "A *you-are-here*."

Fred looked down at his hands. The cuts on his knuckles from the crash were just beginning to heal: He bit the scab off one of them, squeezed out a drop of blood, and put a spot of red to mark where they were.

"That's disgusting!" said Con. "Good idea!"

Fred grinned. "Let's go down," he said. "There's honey for lunch."

He swung down from the tree faster than he should have. A lot of skin got left on a knot of bark halfway down, and he got poked in the eye by a branch. Con followed more slowly, whispering instructions to herself.

Honey was seeping through his shirt as he thumped the last two feet to the forest floor, but his heart was bounding.

"You're alive!" said Max. He threw his arms around Fred's legs and tried to bite his knee in celebration. "We were just thinking we were going to get to eat you."

"Try not to sound so disappointed," said Fred, grinning.

Con reached the lowest branch of the tree. She hesitated, readying for the jump. Lila held out a hand, but Con ignored it and thumped to the forest floor.

"We made a discovery," she said grandly.

"Really? What is it? Food?" asked Lila.

"Wait and see. Let's get to the clearing first," said Con. Then, as if a valve had been released inside her, she let out a cough that was half laughter and half triumph. "I'd never actually climbed a tree before!"

"Never?" said Lila. "Then, that was actually quite amazing."

"I know," said Con. "I think so, too."

As soon as they reached the den, Fred pulled off his shirt and scraped off the honey onto wide leaves.

He crossed to the pool and splashed water on his chest and shirt; bark and dust had stuck to the honey and made a surprisingly tenacious paste.

"Hurry up, Fred!" called Max.

Fred gave up and pulled his sticky shirt on again, and ran back to the den. Lila was turning the tobacco pouch over with careful hands. Baca was hanging around her throat like a necklace, sniffing her collarbone.

"It's red," said Lila. "Tobacco pouches are usually brown."

"So?" asked Con.

Lila leaned forward, her eyes shining. "Bees can't see the color red: They see it as black. What if someone wanted the bees to protect the pouch from other animals? The bees can't see it's not just part of the tree, so they wouldn't have been suspicious."

"Do bees feel suspicious?" said Con skeptically.

Lila flushed. "It's just an idea. But Mama says, in the jungle, you should avoid red; it's a poison color. Whoever owned this would have counted on that. They must have been planning to come back for it."

Fred felt an electric shiver pass over his skin. "There's more. Keep looking."

"A map?" Lila unfolded the paper on a wide flat stone. "What's the *X*?"

"We couldn't see," said Con. "It was too far."

"Maybe treasure?" said Lila. "Maybe a secret tribe?"

"Cannonballs!" said Max.

"Don't!" said Con.

"Or maybe he didn't know what it was; maybe it's just where he was going," said Fred. "I wonder if he knew—"

Max laid one small hand over Fred's mouth. "I'm hungry. Are we going to eat the honey?"

The honey worked on them like medicine. Lila sat up straighter. Color came into Con's cheeks. The taste of the honey was absolutely astonishing: sweet and earthy and wild. It made Fred want to turn backflips across the jungle floor. It was a taste rich enough and deep enough to make them forget, just for half an hour, about the map.

Con

THE NEXT DAY WAS A THURSDAY. THURSDAY at school began with Double Geography; the most exciting thing that happened on Thursday was Biology with old Mr. Martin, who was liable to fart at unexpected intervals.

This Thursday, Fred woke to a rain-forest thunderstorm and rain dripping through the roof of the den into his ear.

Lila and Con were already awake, poring over the map, their heads almost touching. Max was snoring in a rain puddle, mud in his hair and eyebrows. Baca's fur was soaked, slicked down against his bones. He looked as furious as it is possible for a sloth to look.

Lila laid her thumb on the X on the map. "It's got to be much closer than Manaus," she said as she turned, and saw Fred was awake. "And it'd be safer—we'd be on tributaries instead of the main river. Fred! Do you think the raft could get us there?"

Fred moved to look, feeling his muscles creak under his skin. Both girls were shivering. It wasn't cold, but the damp of the day had gotten into their skin.

"We'd have to get through all those weeds, here," he said, "and there's that sign there—"

"That thing that looks like a snake?"

"Exactly." He looked out toward the river and the filing-cabinet-gray sky. "But, yes—I'd say we could."

"But you don't think we *should*?" asked Con. It was, very clearly, a question that begged the answer no. "We saw from the tree! It was miles!"

"We can't stay here forever," said Fred. He had never wanted anything as much as he wanted to launch the raft down the river to find the X. He needed to know what it was to be an explorer. There was another kind of hunger in his gut that had nothing to do with food: It was terror and possibility, fused together with hope.

"You've got to be joking?" Con looked from Lila to Fred.

"But we have a map," said Lila softly. "We would actually know where we're going this time."

"But you don't know what's at the end of it!" Con's skin was white and red in patches.

"But it's got to be something, or there wouldn't be a map," said Fred.

"But what if the *X* is supposed to mean: Never go here because there are things that will come for you in the dark!?"

"But if the other option is to stay here, I thought you'd want to leave?" said Fred.

"I do want to leave! I hate it here!" she spat. "I hate the mosquitoes and the ants and the bites and the endless, endless hunger all the time! But I don't want to follow a map to nowhere—I just want to go home."

Max jerked awake and begin to whine, tugging at Lila's sleeve. She shook him off.

"I want to go home too!" said Lila. Her eyebrows were a tight angry line across her forehead. "But it's no worse for you than for anyone else."

"Yes, it *is*." Con's face was contorted beyond recognition. "You don't understand. It's easier for you because you're used to it! You're from here!"

Lila's eyes widened. "I live in a *city*." Her voice was thin with shock. "We have a *dining room*! With silver candlesticks! I do not live in the jungle!"

"But you're not feeling sick all the time." Con's jaw was clenched. "I wake up every morning feeling like I'm going to vomit!" She thumped the wet ground, and flecks of mud sprang up around her fist.

"But so do I! I want—"

"I hate it so much here I can't breathe—"

"Do you think any of us like it?"

"But you're not alone!" Con burst out. "You've got Max!"

"Exactly! Exactly, and he cries all the time and if he dies it'll be my fault!"

Max heard and let out a roar. Sobs shook his whole body. Fred caught his wrist and held it, to stop him from running.

"At least you know if you die there'll be someone who's bothered to care!" Con yelled over the noise.

"It's not my fault if nobody cares about you," spat Lila. "You don't know—"

"Stop it!" shouted Max. He ran at the two girls and kicked out at both of them, his shoes smacking mud against their skin. "Stop it now!"

Lila's mouth shut with a snap. She turned to her brother, allowed him to climb into her arms. She rubbed his back, her eyes utterly exhausted. "Don't cry. It just makes it worse."

A tear was running down Con's cheek. Fred pulled down a leaf from the wall of the shelter and handed it to her. She mopped her face with it. It didn't do much good. "I'm just so tired," she said. "And I'm so hungry. And I ache."

Lila looked down at her hands. "I didn't mean it, what I just said."

There was a silence. The rain thumped against the leaves over their heads.

"I have nightmares, about my mama," said Lila. "I dream that she's looking for me, and I'm caught in a tree and I can't shout and I can't make her look up and see me." She hesitated. "Do you dream about your parents?"

Fred dreamed of nothing else: his father just out of earshot, just out of reach, while he struggled in the dark to brush him with his fingertips. He half nodded, carefully noncommittal.

Con's mouth shaped a word, then fell still. At last she said, "It's not like that, for me. I live with my great-aunt."

"What happened to your parents?" asked Lila.

"They're dead." Con's mouth hardened again, and

she set her jaw, as if daring them to sympathize. "My father was killed in the war, and then my mother died when I was three. And then a family fostered me."

"But you just said—"

"They had a baby of their own, and they threw me out. So I was sent to live with my great-aunt." Con gave a carefully nonchalant shrug. "She didn't really want me, but there were no other options."

"They kicked you out?"

"They said I bullied the baby. I *didn't*. But I once . . . once it was crying, and it wouldn't stop, and I gave it a tiny slap."

"Oh," said Lila. Her face was stricken.

"And—I don't know." Con paused, swallowed, bit a slither off her thumbnail, went on. "They said I shouted things at the baby. It was only once, truly. And it didn't understand, so why would it matter?"

Fred nodded.

"My great-aunt—she sends me to spend summers with the nuns."

"Nuns?"

"Convent school. That's why I'm in Brazil. The year before that I was in India. She says the travel will improve my character. I hate it."

"Do you want to be improved?" Lila seemed to be trying not to sound too skeptical.

Con tried to smile. "Not really. But she likes girls to be quiet and proper; she says I'm rude. I don't mean to be. But then, when I try to be good—what I think's good—she doesn't notice. Or maybe she doesn't care. So mostly I just . . . I don't know. Don't bother." She wiped her nose with her finger and thumb. "And I don't think . . . I don't think she'll have sent people to look for me. There isn't much money. The convent school paid for my boat fare over here. They have a fund for war orphans." She grimaced, a deep, bitter wince away from her own words. "Charity case."

"So when you said—"

"I lied."

"Your aunt sounds absolutely awful," said Lila.

"Really," said Fred, "she does." He wondered if he should punch Con on the arm, the way the other boys did at school. He decided it might not be a punching occasion.

"She's just old, really." Con breathed in a deep, shuddering breath, as if she had expelled something weighty. She scrubbed at her eye with a handful of her hair. "I've never told anyone. About my foster family. Please don't tell anyone."

"Who would we tell?" said Fred, looking at the green hush of the jungle around them.

Lila unhooked Baca's claws from her hair, and settled him on Con's shoulder. "Here. He might try to eat your ears. But he means it in a nice way." A tear ran down Con's cheek. Baca licked it away.

Fred looked at Con. Fred never hugged anybody. His father did not believe in hugging; he said it was presumptuous and unhygienic. But Con looked so suddenly bony, and defeated. He made a fist and pushed it softly against Con's shoulder, rocking her sideways.

Con waited longer than Fred had expected before she tensed up and, with a half laugh, shook him off.

"Okay," she said. Her breath was shaky. "Fine. You win. We'll follow the map."

Fred felt something fierce and hot ignite in his stomach. "If we gather grubs and berries today," he said, "we could be ready to go by tomorrow."

Lila looked at Con's tense face. "Tomorrow," she said.

Con hunched her shoulders and bent her head. It was almost a nod.

Smoke

THE NEXT DAY DAWNED SWELTERINGLY HOT;
all four woke slick with sweat, with dragonflies
trying to drink from their skin.

For breakfast Con found a banana tree, and they
made a sack from Max's vest and filled it until bananas
poked out of the neck. They gorged on unripe bananas
until Max was sick on his own shoes.

After breakfast a wind began to pick up. It was a very
welcome breeze on Fred's face as he prepared the raft,
double-checking every knot.

It was the same wind that nearly killed them.

Fred and Lila were crouched on the raft in the river,
testing how it moved under their weight, retying vines.
Con and Max were hunting for berries to add to their
provisions. Baca was half in, half out of Lila's pocket,
sniffing the breeze. A swirl of air reached them from

the jungle, and Baca let out a mew. A shiver passed down Fred's spine.

"Does something smell odd to you?"

Baca seemed nervous. He began trying to bite Lila's hem into ribbons.

Lila stared back toward the path to their clearing. Where there should have been shards of green sunlight, there was a swirl of gray. "Is that . . . dust?"

"It's smoke," said Fred. He sniffed again. "It's a fire!"

For a moment they both stared, paralyzed, at the billowing gray. Then Lila let out a scream, and the scream shook the whole raft. "Max! Where's Max!"

"He was right there, on the bank, with Con!" The smoke began to flow like water, sweeping out of the trees toward them. Fred's eyes stung.

There was a pounding of feet and Con came sprinting out of the bushes, her hair flying behind her, catching in the trees. She half dived, half fell into the river and swam, splashing frantically, toward the raft.

"I just saw it!" she hauled herself up over the edge. "The clearing's on fire! It's horrible!" Her eyes were red and wild. She stared around. "Where's Max?"

"I thought he was with you!" Lila's face was unrecognizable.

"What? No! He said he was going to find you—he wanted to play with Baca!"

"No! This can't be happening!" Lila stood up on the raft. "Max!"

"Max!" shouted Fred. "Max!"

"I'm here!" The voice was tiny, and thin, and sounded of pure panic.

Max had scrambled up a tree. He was sitting, whimpering, unable to scream, in the branches overhanging the river. Fred stared up at him, divided between shock and terror.

"How did he get up there?" said Con. "It's so high!"

"Jump in, Max! Jump into the water!" called Lila.

"I can't!"

"Max! I am ordering you!" Her voice was shrill, wire thin. "I'm your big sister and you do what I say!"

Max's voice was a shriek. "I *can't*!" He began crying in long, wordless screams, balanced above the river.

Fred began pulling off his boots, but Lila thrust Baca at Con, hitched up her skirt, and was in the water. Fred had never seen a human swim so fast. She scrambled up the bank, her nails tearing against the mud, and sprinted for the tree.

She began climbing, hauling herself up with just her arms where the footholds failed.

"Max!" she called. "Just stay there!"

Fred and Con sat on the raft below, Con holding Baca in both hands, watching, coughing as the smoke thickened around them.

Max was crouching like a sloth, with his arms and legs wrapped around the branch. Fred squinted up to see Lila crawling along the branch, talking to him, coaxing him, trying to untangle him, her whole body shaking as she moved. Max had stopped crying and was now rigid faced, and completely silent, which was somehow more frightening than the screaming.

The first flames appeared, snaking along the path from the clearing. The heat sent up sparks, catching at Lila's skin and Max's feet. There was a bang, like an erupting paper bag, as below them seed pods exploded in the heat.

"Jump in!" Fred shouted wildly. "Just jump in and we'll come and get you!"

There was only smoke now: smoke and the sound

of Lila calling to Max, singing to him, coaxing him desperately.

"Jump!" shrieked Con. "Please, now!"

Then two bodies plummeted down into the river. The water closed over them.

They landed in an eddy of water, and the current swept the two of them, too fast, into the middle of the river where there were rapids.

Fred squinted through the smoke. Their heads did not resurface. "Take the pole," he said to Con. He took a deep breath. "And if we all die, tell my dad . . . sorry." He dived headfirst into the brown water and struck out toward the rapids.

Fred opened his eyes, but all he could see was churning foam. A body smashed into his and he grabbed it; it was Max. He tried, through his panic, to remember what he had read about saving people from drowning. You had to gently cup their chin in your hand—he remembered that clearly. But *how?* The current was too fast to make cupping of any kind seem plausible. Fred spun onto his back and hauled Max up to lie on his stomach, trying to keep the boy's head out of the water. He couldn't tell if Max was breathing. With one arm, he began to swim backward toward the bank. The water was trying to pull them under; he could see only smoke and spray, and the river sweeping over his face with every other stroke.

"Don't panic," he whispered to himself. This would be a bad moment to panic.

A burning branch fell into the water inches away from them. Max gave a cough, and spat out a water beetle, hacking weakly, as the water washed over them again.

Just as Fred was starting to feel that panicking was really the only available option, he saw something in the smoke. A yell came over the sound of the fire and the water in his ears. "Fred! Max!"

It was Con.

"Over here!" he called.

"Swim toward me!" she screamed.

"I can't! The current!" It was bitterly hard work staying in one place; one of his legs was starting to cramp, and he was terrified that Max's head would go under the water.

A shape came out of the smoke: It was the raft. Con was covered in gray ash; she was paddling hard with both hands, roaring their names as she came.

She reached Fred just as he hit a swirl in the

current. There was water in his eyes and a painful cracking as Fred's ear smacked against the wood and a scream from Con, a great scrambling and a burning in his muscles, but then Fred was kneeling on the raft, coughing up water, and Max was there, spitting and vomiting up water and leaves and pineapple.

"Where's Lila?" asked Con. Her voice was wild and high. "Where's Lila?"

"I couldn't see her!"

Fred choked out a mouthful of water and crawled to the edge of the raft. He tried to draw in a deep enough breath to dive in again, but each gasp for air made him gag.

There was a great lurch, and they tipped sideways. Two hands appeared, then Lila's face, her chin on the edge of the raft.

"Lila!" Fred let out a noise he hadn't known he was capable of—something between a roar and a whoop—and grabbed her wrists, then her shoulders, heaving her to the center of the raft. She lay panting. She had a cut across the bridge of her nose, and blood ran down over her mouth and chin, but she was alive.

"M-Max," she gasped.

"He's here, he's fine!" Con was shouting, though her

head was next to Lila's. "Just breathe. He's fine, I swear."

She pushed with the pole, thrusting the raft to the side of the river where the current flowed steadily, propelling them away from the flames. At last, when the air was clear and the fire was crackling in the distance, she guided the raft into the shallows, where it stilled, swaying on the water.

A crowd of blue butterflies alighted on the bank next to them. Max was wearing pond weed on his head like a tiara. Lila cradled him in her arms. He cradled Baca. Baca cradled Max's thumb.

It was a long time before anybody spoke.

"What happens now?" said Lila. "Do we go back?"

"I don't know. Everything was burned," said Con. She was still shivering with shock, and although the sun was warm, the hairs along her arm were standing on end. "I saw it."

"The den? And the bees?"

"Everything. The whole clearing." Con wiped the ash from her face. She looked like a panda bear. "It must have been our fire. We should have left someone to watch it. The embers were too hot."

Fred spoke quietly. "So we follow the map."

"Wait—wasn't the map in your pocket?" asked Lila.

Ice swamped Fred's gut. "Oh," he said. "Oh no." He reached into his pocket and fished out the red leather pouch.

The ink on the map had run so badly that it was no more than a blackish smudge. The paper itself was pulp, and as he passed it to Lila, it tore in two.

He swallowed. "Sorry," he whispered.

Lila looked as though she might cry. "Don't be," she said.

There was an impatient tut behind them—a sort of *chuff*—and the sound of scratching. "You're both so defeatist," said Con. She had pulled a flint from her pocket, and as they watched, she tore a strip of bark from the raft and began etching something on it.

"There—that was the squiggle—and that was where the river curved," she said.

"Your photogenic memory!" said Max.

"Photographic," said Con. She kept scratching. "There," she said. "What do you think? Does that look right?"

Fred studied her map. "It does look almost exactly—"

"Not almost exactly. Exactly," said Con sharply. "I was just being polite, actually. I *know* it's right."

Fred looked at the bark, and then up at Lila, at Max,

at Con. "Whatever it is that's on the map, it's got to be better than what's back there. What do you say?"

That same feeling—fear, and possibility, and something that felt like what his father called "sheer bloody-mindedness"—began to churn inside his stomach.

Con bit her lip. Then, without a word, she took up the pole again, and pushed the raft off the bank, back into the river and the corridor of dappled green light. "Left at the next fork?" she asked.

"Left at the next fork," said Lila.

They coasted onward for that whole day. Some of the tributaries were only eight feet across, with a cathedral roof of branches above them creating a midnight darkness; others were so wide and bright it was hard to see the opposite shore.

As the sky grew pink, Fred turned and saw, on the opposite bank, a caiman as big as a Great Dane. It lay in mud, its eyes at half-mast, staring straight ahead. His heart clenched.

"What do we do?" hissed Con. She spoke without moving a single facial muscle.

"Nothing," said Lila. Fred held the pole in his

hands like a spear. But the caiman did not move as they floated past.

The sun dipped lower over the river ahead of them. The light grew purplish and thin.

"We're not safe, are we?" asked Con.

"No," said Fred. "But we could pretend we are."

Lila tightened her grip on Baca's paw. "Let's act as if the river's on our side. Let's act as if the jungle wants us to win."

The stars began to come out, turning the water deep black under a silver-flecked sky.

"Even if rivers don't take sides?"

"Even then."

On the River

I T WAS ALMOST COMPLETELY DARK WHEN THEY found somewhere to moor, a place where the bank didn't rise too steeply from the river, and where the trees didn't look so much like an army ranged on the bank. Lila steered the raft toward the land, and Fred jumped ashore.

"I'll check there aren't any caiman marks," he said.

"I'll come too," said Con.

"No," said Max. He gripped her ankle. "Stay."

Con flushed, and swallowed a smile. She stayed. Fred walked through patches of trees, his heart beating in his ears, swinging a stick ahead of him through ferns, sniffing, watching his feet, searching for the smell of anything recently killed. But it smelled only of growing things, and of resin and birds.

"It's fine!" he called. "It's safe!" His voice twisted,

echoing through the trees to reach the others, and they shouted instructions back to him and to each other and pushed the raft ashore.

It didn't occur to anybody not to trust one another now, he thought. They had become a pack. Or, an expedition, he corrected himself. That was what you called a group of explorers.

They slept that night on the forest floor, their backs touching. Though the day had been heavy with sun, the night was cloudless and cold, and Fred slept with his knees tucked up into his shirt. He found it was unexpectedly reassuring now to feel Max's foot near his nose when he turned in the night. When the nightmares came, it was good to be able to hear the others breathing.

They traveled on for another day and another night, the river carrying them at its own pace on its silver back. None of them spoke much. They watched the sides of the banks, waiting, alert, tense.

On the morning of the third day, it started to rain. Max, who had been staring out at the green, began to scream.

"Sharks! Lila! Sharks!"

Lila grabbed Max's wrist. "Hold on to me," she said.

Fred looked around. There was only the great expanse of water and the thrum of falling rain.

"There are no sharks in the Amazon, Max," he said. "It's okay." As the words were leaving his mouth, he saw what Max had seen: a fin, rising up out of the water.

Con screamed. Lila let out a hiss. Fred froze. He said, speaking through rigid jaw, "Max. Come away from the side of the raft."

Then the fin dipped, disappeared, and out from the water leaped an arc of pinkish-gray body, curving against the rain and the thunder-colored sun.

"A dolphin!" said Lila. Her whole face was transformed.

Fred rubbed his eyes, and looked again; but he hadn't imagined it. The dolphin was pink.

The arc of pink was followed by another, dipping so that the half curve of its back rose out of the water, and another, and then a puff of water from a dolphin's blowhole. They were coming closer.

"Shall we jump in?" asked Fred. "Do you think they'd let us swim with them?"

"Don't!" said Con. "There might be piranha!"

The pod of dolphins circled the raft at a distance. There were five of them, Fred thought, or possibly six.

One leaped up, clean out of the water, only six feet away.

Max clapped and squealed. "Shh!" said Lila. "We have to be quiet, Maxie. They're deciding if they trust us."

It did seem that this was what the dolphins were doing: There was something speculative in the way they swam closer, doubled back and away, and closer again. Then, without warning, the pod turned and began to swim away. The rain grew thicker.

Fred's heart lurched. He couldn't bear to see them go. He pulled off his shoes, stood, and dived in, striking hard for the disappearing dolphins.

As he neared them, four of the dolphins sped up and ducked deeper into the water, but one turned. Fred trod water; he held out his hand.

He tried to stay as still as he could. The dolphin swam up to him, a shape approaching under the surface. He gasped, and spat out water. It was rose gray, and covered in deep scars along its back. Its snout was lined with fierce-looking teeth, but its eyes were steady and soft.

Fred tried to steady his breathing. It was the most astonishing thing he had ever seen; it was like a battered river god. He held out his hand again.

"Hello," he whispered. "I'm Fred."

The dolphin dipped its nose to Fred's hand. He gasped at the surprising roughness of its skin. It butted his hand, then huffed as if disappointed and ducked down deep under the surface. Fred watched, expecting its shadow to disappear. But as he turned back to the raft, the dolphin erupted from the water in front of him. It leaped clean over his head, showering him with spray, dipped down again, and disappeared.

The others were shouting and beckoning from the raft. They hauled him up, all three trying to grab him at once.

Fred couldn't speak; he didn't want to. He needed the memory to be sharp, carbon copied onto his heart and lungs. He imagined his father's face when he told him. His heart sang and thrummed in his chest. But the others were boiling over with questions and ideas.

"It was like it trusted you!" said Con.

"Or, maybe it thought you were going to feed it?" said Lila.

"Maybe someone was feeding them those sardines?" said Fred.

. . .

Later that day, just as Fred's head was beginning to swim with hunger, Lila spotted a fig tree on the shore. Fred climbed up and shook the fruit down onto the raft. They tied up the sleeves and neck of his shirt and made it into a sack. Max counted as he put them in: "A hundred and twelvety!" he said, triumphant.

Behind him, Lila mouthed, "Fifty-three."

"I always hated figs at school," said Con. "I thought they tasted like eating someone else's snot—but, actually, they're the best thing in the world."

Max fished a handful of figs out of the sack and pushed them into his pocket. "These ones are mine. I doesn't like sharing," he said haughtily.

Lila fed one of the figs to Baca, who ate it hungrily and, half an hour later, pooed lavishly over her lap.

She laughed, and washed her skirt off over the edge of the raft. "Sloths only go to the bathroom about once a week," she said, "so at least it's done for a few days."

Baca looked thin and even more wide eyed than usual. "They poo half their body weight each time," she said.

"That sounds . . . stressful," said Con.

The surface of the raft was constantly being washed with river water, so she draped the clean skirt over her shoulders to dry, traveling down the river like a floating scarecrow. Fred's shoes and shorts grew sodden, but his upper half remained bone dry.

The sun was hotter than two days put together. Con's cheeks and forehead grew bright pink with sunburn. Lila made her a cold compress out of weeds and braided leaves, which leaked green water down over her eyebrows but eased some of the burning.

That night, as they lay on a bed of fallen leaves, Baca moved across Lila's shoulder, sniffed at her neck, and climbed up Fred's calf. Sloths are nocturnal, and Baca seemed unusually sprightly by sloth standards. He fastened his arms and legs around Fred's knee, and began to chew at his shorts.

Fred lay still, trying not to move his leg, looking up at the stars. They broke out in spirals and galloping animals and clustered like hordes of white butterflies ranging across the night.

Lila was watching too. "Fred?" she whispered. "Are you awake?"

"Yes," he whispered back.

"The moon's so close." She sounded half asleep. "You could wear it as a hat."

Fred nodded in the darkness but didn't speak.

"At home," she whispered, "you only ever get small squares of sky—however much you can fit between buildings and church spires."

"Yes," whispered Fred. "I've never seen anything like this."

Lila's voice grew even quieter. "Fred? Are we going to be okay?"

He kept staring up at the sky. "I don't know."

Con stirred, and turned to look at them. "Are you scared?" she whispered.

"Yes," said Fred. He had never been so frightened in his life. But they were alive. He held that thought in his fist, tight against his skin.

"Me too," Lila said. "Don't tell Max."

"Me too," whispered Con. She gave a grunt of disgust. "But that's obvious. I can't work out how to hide it like you do."

They lay, breathing close to one another. "When this is over," said Lila, "let's all swear to meet somewhere."

"Where?" asked Con.

"Where's the most famous place to eat in London?"

"The Ritz?" said Fred.

"Then we'll meet there," said Lila, "and we'll have one of every single kind of cake, and this will be like a dream."

"And hot chocolate," murmured Max. He sounded three-quarters asleep.

"Max," said Lila, twisting to touch his forehead, "go back to sleep."

Fred stole a look at the other three. Con had closed her eyes. Her brow was furrowed, but her lips had half a smile at the tips.

On the fourth day, the river began to change. The trees arched densely overhead, and the water was choked with weeds. It no longer smelled fresh. Fish flitted through the reeds.

"Are they—piranhas?" said Con. "I mean, piranha?"

Lila peered down over the edge of the raft and nodded, her jaw set. She stroked Baca, hanging around her neck, and buried her chin in his fur. Her breath, as she exhaled, was shaky.

It was midmorning, but it grew dark as the branches thickened above them.

"Is it just me, or does the river feel suddenly less on our side?" asked Con.

"Not just you," said Fred shortly. His upper lip and forehead were dripping sweat, the sweat not only from the work of poling. But he had Con's bark map in his pocket, and the thought of it warmed his chest, beating back against the cold doubt in his stomach.

The current was in their favor, but traveling through the weeds was arm-aching, back-stretching, skin-shredding work.

"Watch out!" called Lila.

Fred flinched, looking around for something about to hit him in the face, and then watched, in silence, as a snake slipped along a branch, spiraled up the trunk of a tree, and disappeared into the green over their heads. Even Max didn't move.

"It's almost certainly not deadly!" said Fred. He winced. He'd intended it to sound reassuring, but instead his voice had landed somewhere between "desperate lying" and "stern aunt on a deathbed."

He concentrated on poling, doubling his speed until they were past the weeds and were speeding down the dark-green passageway of overhanging trees.

"We're close," said Fred. "On the map this river goes on until a lake—I think it would be three or four hours, but it's hard to tell—and then there's a black square, and then a short line—that might be a path or a river, but it could just be a squiggle—and then the *X*."

Con stretched into the water for a broad stick as it

floated by and began to paddle. "The sooner we get there, the sooner we'll know the worst."

The raft followed the river, Fred's pole splashing in his impatience to see what was around the next corner. He guided the raft around a great floating fallen tree, traversed another five minutes of dark water, and found, without warning, that they had come to the mouth of a small lake.

The lake was an exquisite blue, shining under a cloudless sky, but Fred did not notice. They all four sat crouched on the raft, looking up, their jaws open and their eyes wide.

There was a long silence.

Then Lila spoke. "Did I ever mention I'm terrified of heights?"

At the Top of the Cliff

A GREAT CLIFF ROSE UP FROM THE JUNGLE, covered in vines. It was fifty times as tall as Fred. The rock face would have been gray, but it was so covered in foliage that it seemed to rise from the earth like a growing thing, a great green extension of the jungle floor.

"*That's* what the black square meant," breathed Fred.

"Oh *no*," breathed Con. "I don't want to do this."

Lila's hand, clutching Baca on her shoulder, was shaking. "Fred? Could you climb that?"

Fred swallowed. "Definitely," he lied. He stared at the great green expanse. It would be like climbing a green cathedral, he thought. "We all could. There'll be so many handholds; it'll be like climbing a ladder."

"Max can't climb ladders," said Lila.

"Then one of us will strap him to our back with lianas," said Fred.

"I just don't think—," began Con.

But Fred had never wanted anything as much as he wanted to know what was at the top of that rock. "Where would we go if we turn back now?" he said.

Lila bit down on one of her braids. Her jaw was rigid with fear, but her gaze was steady. "We've got to try, haven't we? There might be someone up there who can take us home."

They moored the raft and picked their way through the jungle toward the rock. The trees grew so thickly they had to force their way between them, and even though it was barely three hundred feet, it took fully half an hour of hauling Max over tree trunks and navigating under branches lined with vicious thorns.

Fred stood at the foot of the cliff and laid a hand on it. The rock was warm to touch, and uneven—*Good for finding handholds,* he thought. The vines that coated it looked strong. He tugged on a handful of thin lianas; they did not tear.

"See? It'll just be like climbing the rope at school, in gym lessons," he said. "It'll be simple!"

"I hate climbing the rope," said Con. "So, no, actually, it's not *simple*."

"I could go up by myself," said Fred, "and shout down what's up there?"

Lila shook her head. She looked suddenly much older than the rest of them, and stern.

"You never split up in unfamiliar territory," she said. "We're coming with you." She unwound Baca from the crook of her elbow and settled him securely on the back of her neck, looping her braid around his body to keep him moored. "But I can't carry Max. We'd both die."

"I can take him on my back." Fred tried to banish any hint of doubt from his voice.

"Doesn't Max get to choose? Max says he won't," said Max.

"No," said Lila. The stern look became sterner. "You don't get to choose. I almost *never* make you do things you don't want to at home, Max. But you have to do this."

"No!"

"Yes! We're going to tie you onto Fred with ropes so you won't fall. And you can cry if you want to, but it won't help," she said, as Max began to sob.

Max did not make the climbing easier. His mutinous weight threw Fred's normal climbing rhythm off, and it was a very slow ascent. He breathed loudly into Fred's ear, and got spit in his hair, and he was heavy. Fred was aching before they were halfway up. He went first, with Con and Lila following his handholds. Twice, he went the wrong way, and had to shout down apologies as he retreated and moved sideways, agonizingly slowly, with Max's feet digging into his ribs.

"You have to shift backward—but don't look down!" he called to the girls.

"We already did," Con called back. Her voice was strangled with nerves. "It wasn't a good idea."

Fred shook a beetle off his eye and gripped another handful of vines. He hauled upward. At last, inch by inch, the roots of trees growing down the rock came into sight; then the tip of the rock curved and became an incline with bushes, which became flat land. Fred let out a yell of triumph.

Con and Lila followed. Con crawled to the nearest tree and spat a mouthful of bile and saliva into the roots.

"I can't . . . believe . . . we just did that," she gasped.

Lila untied Max, and gripped him tight in her

arms. She was still shaking. "We did it!" she whispered in his ear. "Think about how proud Mama and Papa would be."

"Can we tell them?"

"As soon as we get home." Their heads were close together, suddenly a pair set apart, and Fred thought, for the first time, how very similar they looked, how Lila's eyes were Max's eyes, and his mouth, her mouth.

"We're so close now," said Fred. "This is the squiggle, I think."

There was something in front of them that looked like it might be a path, or an animal trail, or just an illusion. They hacked through the foliage. An uncomfortable amount of it was knee-high bushes with spikes. Fred's knees became flecked with blood. The ground grew marshy, and tiny flying insects mobbed them, swarming into Fred's mouth and up his nose.

Con snorted like a horse, waving both hands in front of her face. "Is it far?" she asked, turning to look at Fred. "I don't know how much of this I can take."

But even as she spoke, the ground gave way.

It dropped suddenly down, smooth moss on smooth stone. She didn't have time to stop and cascaded down it on her back, thumping against stones and roots. Fred launched himself after her, scrabbling to stay upright and grabbing at trees; Lila and Max followed, Max on his backside, gasping in shock.

They tumbled into a heap at the bottom. Fred's chin connected with someone's ankle. He shoved the ankle away and brushed leaves out of his eyes. Lila scooped Baca into her arms, and took hold of Max's elbow.

They stood with their backs to a slope, at the edge of a vast expanse of stone.

It was an enormous stone courtyard, as wide as a hay field and at least four times as long. The ground was built from white and yellow stone blocks, rough hewn and smooth at the top, as from the passing of many thousands of feet. It was set in a slight dip in the ground, so the earth rose up from it on all sides, forming a natural wall. Down the middle of the great stone courtyard grew two rows of trees, creating a boulevard. There were heaps of stone in five or six places, as if small houses had lined each side.

"My God," breathed Lila.

Fred took a step forward. Among the trees he could see half-formed stone pillars, some waist high, some taller than he was. High, high overhead was a thick canopy of green, forming a roof over the stones.

"Look!" said Fred. "Over there!"

At the far end of the stone expanse there was a vast stone wall, half crumbling and covered in passion-fruit vines. Lining the wall were four immense sculptures, hewn out of wood and stone, taller than two men. They were crumbling, and the stone had fallen away, but it was possible to see what they had been: a monkey, a panther, a woman, and a man.

"It's a *city*," breathed Lila.

The sudden thump of a footstep made Fred spin around, bending, as he had done once days before, for something to throw.

A man strode from behind one of the stone pillars. He was pointing a knife at them.

"Whatever you were thinking of doing," he said, "I would advise against it."

The Ruined City

THE MAN WAS TALL. HIS ARMS AND HANDS were covered in scars and burns; old white scars crisscrossed with new red ones. He held the knife at the level of their necks casually, as if it were a bread stick.

"Like the Minotaur," whispered Con.

At the man's side, close at his heels, waddled an enormous vulture with a red head and a curved beak. Its head came up higher than the man's knees.

"That small person in the dolorous trouser suit." The man's nostrils had a high flare to them, and they twitched as he spoke. His voice was deep. His accent, Fred thought, belonged among good tailoring and fast motorcars. "What's wrong with him?"

There was silence, except for Max's sobs.

"Well?" said the man. He twirled the knife in his fingers.

"He's crying," said Fred.

"Why? He sounds like a dying screech owl. Like a lion blowing on a ship's whistle."

Fred's heart was red hot and beating double time. He was surprised that his voice sounded so almost calm. "He's five."

"That's not a reason."

"You're pointing a knife at his head," said Lila.

"That's not a *good* reason." But he lowered the knife.

The man stepped closer, into a patch of green sun, and they could see him more clearly.

His dress was exquisite but smelled pungent. His trousers, Fred saw, were quite ordinary—green khaki, worn through at the knee and spotlessly clean—but that, along with a white shirt, torn off at the elbow and patched with coconut fiber, was the only thing about him that was normal. His shoes were made from what looked like alligator skin, with very thin vines for shoelaces. A jacket, sewn neatly from black furs, hung over his shoulders. The buttons were caiman teeth. He wore leather cuffs on each wrist, a signet ring on his little finger.

From a distance, he might have been on his way to a country house party. Up close, he looked as though he had reconstructed a prime minister from once-living things.

Con swallowed. She spoke in a whisper. "Is it just me, or does he look like the kind of person who won't definitely not kill you?" Her eyes were stretched open and her skin was taut over her bones.

Fred's entire body had gone rigid, but he managed to nod his head half an inch. He spoke out of the corner of his mouth. "Not just you."

The man took another step toward them; his right foot swung slightly out to the side as he moved. Fred noticed for the first time that the man's right leg was strapped with three slim, highly polished pieces of wood. Despite the limp and the scars and the stubble, the animal Fred thought of was a panther. Something with strong jaws and sharp manners.

"Who are you?" said the man.

None of the children answered. They looked at one another. Nobody wanted to be the first to speak.

"How did you get here?" asked the man impatiently.

Fred took a deep breath. "Our plane crashed," he said, "and the pilot died. And we followed a map." He put his hands in his pockets, trying to look nonchalant, trying to find something he could fight with if he needed to. He could feel only a handful of squashed *açaí* berries, which would not be very deadly in a battle.

"Show me."

Fred handed him the scrap of bark, fumbling in his back pocket embarrassingly, his fingers suddenly uncooperative and clumsy.

The man glanced at it. "Who drew this?"

Silently, Con raised her hand.

"Based on what?"

Con shook her head so that her hair fell in a protective wave across her face.

"Well?" said the man.

"We found a map in a tree," said Fred, "and Con made a copy, when it got wet."

The man screwed up the bark in his hand.

"Please," said Lila. "Don't be angry. All we wanted to do was get home."

The man looked down at the vulture, as if for inspiration. "And what am I supposed to do with you now?"

"Nothing! Just let us stay for a little? We won't make any noise," said Lila.

"That small one will."

Max felt the man's gaze fall on him, and he began to cry again. The man let out a sound that was somewhere between a sigh and a growl.

Lila picked Max up. "Sorry." Her voice wavered, and Baca caught the fear from her skin and let out a mew like a cat. "He's only five," she whispered.

"You all keep saying that as if it's an explanation. Should I *like* him simply because he's small? I do not like undercooked food. Children are just undercooked people."

Con's lip began to quiver. Fred looked at her, surprised—but he moved his shoe half an inch, so that their feet touched.

The man looked at them, ranged in a line in front of him, shaking with nerves and longing. He sighed.

"Are you thirsty?" he asked.

"Yes," said Fred.

"Very," said Lila.

"Very, very," said Max. He sniffed tearfully and wiped a wedge of snot on his wrist.

"Wait here." He glared at Max. "Don't touch the vulture. He bites when he's anxious, and it takes very little to make him anxious. Vultures have nervous souls."

The man strode across the great stone courtyard.

He stopped at a tree trunk, a stump of wood as wide as a well, and lifted a slab of stone off the top of it. Fred shielded his eyes and stared; the tree trunk had been hollowed out and was full of water. The man dipped a large green bowl into the water and stomped back to them.

"Here." He thrust the bowl at Fred. The ring on the man's finger was not gold, Fred saw; it was bone, coated in flakes of iridescent snake scales.

Fred looked at the bowl in his hands. It was made from an explorer's pith helmet, the brim of the hat bent into a lip. Fred sniffed it. The man raised his eyebrows.

"I assure you it's perfectly clean," he said.

Fred took a gulp. Thankfully, it didn't taste of hair, only a little of wood, birds, and the rain forest. He drank deeply, and passed it to Lila, who handed it to Max, who dunked his whole head in the hat.

The man waited until all four had drunk. Then he took back the bowl and offered it to the vulture.

As the vulture drank, the man rested his hand on the bird's head and stroked its wattle with his thumb. His face was tense. "What is it that you want?" he said.

The children looked at one another.

"We want you to help us get home," said Lila. She

spoke very quietly, so quietly he had to bend down to hear.

"And why should I?"

"I can't look after Max much longer; he has allergies, and nightmares, and I don't know what I can dress him with if he keeps ripping holes in his clothes. Please help us."

As she spoke, the vulture waddled away from the man's side and headed straight for Max, who was hiccuping and sniffing. A line of snot dripped from Max's nose onto his ankle

The vulture dipped its beak to Max's feet and pecked at the snot; then it wedged its nose into the side of Max's shoe, and breathed in deeply through the holes in its beak.

"What's he doing?" said Max. His eyes were dilated with fear, wide and round as pennies, but he reached down and touched the bald head of the vulture. It snapped its beak. Max snatched his hand back, then, more confidently, returned it to the vulture's head.

The vulture let out a guttural croak. It sounded almost like purring.

Then Max looked up, smiling, at the man. "He's mine now," he said.

The man looked from Max to the vulture and back at Fred and Lila and Con. His face was emotionless, but his eyes were not.

"I shouldn't trust the instincts of that bird," he said. "He probably just thinks the boy smells like meat. But. All right. Come with me."

He led them down the stone boulevard. There was a cascade of questions tumbling through Fred's head: Who was this man? How had he got here? Would he help them? But something in the man's walk did not encourage conversation.

The canopy was so thick overhead that the light filtered a succulent green down into their path. The man led them to a place where blocks of stone and mud had been stacked to make three sides of a storeroom. It was empty but for the shocking blue and green flowers that grew in the cracks. Vines crisscrossed over the top, forming a roof of sorts.

"Here," said the man. "You can sleep here."

"Who built this? Did you?"

"No," he said shortly. "I did not." He looked at the stone floor. "I might make you some reed sleeping mats tonight. If I have time. The vines will shelter you if there's any rain. More or less."

"Thank you," said Fred. Con still hadn't spoken, but she nodded in thanks.

"But beyond the statues, that curtain of lianas—you see?" He pointed. Fred followed his hand and saw, at the far end of the city square, falling from the wall behind the statues, a great swathe of tangling creepers.

They nodded.

"You don't go anywhere near there. Do you understand? That is my private space."

Con tried to speak, but only a strangled burr came out.

"We understand," said Lila.

"I mean it. Keep your word, or I'll cut off your ears and give them to the vulture to wear as a hat."

"Don't!" wailed Max. He put his hands over his ears. "I don't like him!"

"Shh, Max," said Lila. "He's doesn't mean it."

Fred looked at the man. He was fairly sure Lila was right, but it seemed risky to assume, of a man who used teeth for buttons, that he was joking.

Max tugged at the man's trousers. "What time do we eat?"

The man looked down at him, baffled. "Whenever you want."

"Oh—but—we mean, whenever suits you," said Con. Her voice was croaky, but she looked relieved that it had started working again.

"You eat whenever you catch and cook something. That's usually how it works. Unless you don't catch anything."

"But—don't you—you're the adult."

"I'm *an* adult, certainly. Look, there are berries. There may be some bananas on the trees in the west corner, if they weren't eaten by monkeys in the night. And you can hunt."

"But," said Con, "you're the grown-up." Her voice had truly come back now, and she scowled. "Grown-ups cook for children. Those are the rules. That's how it's always been done!"

The man seemed to be losing patience. "My dear." He crouched in front of her, dangerously close. "Which aspect of this"—he waved his hand at the stone towers, at his scaly shoes, at the vulture—"makes you think I would care how things have always been done?"

"But that isn't how it works in the real world!"

"This *is* the real world." He thumped his knuckles on the stone floor. "This, here. The real world is where you feel most real."

"But, who are—," said Fred.

"But, please—," said Lila.

"But, don't you—," said Con. All three reached out, as if to grab him.

"Good lord," said the man. "It's like watching a dog eat a bee. You have six hands between you. Or eight, if you count the small one trying to eat a dragonfly."

"Max!" said Lila. "Stop that!"

"Do you at least have knives?" the man asked.

"We have one between us," said Fred. "We found it." It didn't seem the right moment to explain that, technically, the knife almost certainly belonged to this tall, dark, unexpectedly dressed stranger; he might demand they give it back.

The man sighed. "I'll give you each a flint. Then you can hunt, at least."

He crossed to another stump of tree trunk, lifted a small boulder off its top, and fished something from the hollow space within. "Here. They're already sharpened."

He handed them each a stone, expertly chiseled to the size of a large arrowhead. Fred tested the edge with his thumb. It bit into his skin and a drop of blood ballooned out.

The man raised his eyebrows. "You can use banana leaves as bandages. If you lose any fingers worth eating, give them to the vulture." He handed a stone to Max. "There you are, young cacophony. That one's the sharpest."

"Max is too young for knives," said Lila. She tried to take it from her brother, but he jerked away and held both hands behind his back.

"Is he? How do you know?" said the man. He sounded interested.

"It's just a fact—people don't give little boys knives."

"I feel fairly sure I was given a knife at a young age. And I turned out perfectly normal."

Fred looked at the buttons on the man's shirt; they glinted white and sharp in the sun. He said nothing.

The man sighed. "It's getting late," he said. "You can have something from my own stores—but just tonight. Don't think it's going to be routine. You'll have to hunt for yourselves."

All four let out deep sighs of relief. The man strode back to the hollowed-out trunk and bent to a pile of stones next to the tree stump. Up close, they seemed to be arranged into something more definite than a pile: a rectangle, with wide slabs across the top. The man lifted two of the slabs, reached in, and brought out the body of a bird, plucked but ungutted.

"Caracara," he said. He dropped it into Fred's hands. It was cool and clammy. "They're common as rats here."

"Thank you. Could you tell us how to gut it?" Fred asked tentatively.

"With the flints, boy!"

"But how's the best way? Sir," he added, just in case.

"When the first man learned to cook, he did so without recipe books. He worked it out. *You work it out.*"

They all four stared at him.

He sighed. "Cut along the stomach, scoop out anything that looks too detailed, and cook the rest. As a rule of thumb, with innards, if it would take more than one color to draw it, don't eat it. So, kidneys are fine— all reddish brown, intestines less so, unless you're feeling exceptionally brave."

"But—just quickly, before you go—how do we cook it?" said Lila.

"With fire." He smiled a half smile. "Or that one— the blond one, wearing her face like a weapon in a barroom brawl—could try to cook it by glaring at it."

"Wait!—Please, just a second—" Fred made a last

effort as the man turned to go. "Who are you? What do we call you? What is this place? How did you get here? Are you an explorer? Do you live here? Are you planning to help us? We need to know!"

Fred thought of all the explorers he'd read about— there were so many who had strode into the jungle and never reappeared. Percy Fawcett, and his son Jack. Raleigh Rimell. Christopher Maclaren. He tried to remember what the photographs in the newspapers had looked like.

The man turned to face Fred full on. His face shifted from wry to something darker and harder to trace. "I'm a bush pilot. Not an explorer. I used to ferry supplies back and forth from the smaller towns to Manaus. I crashed here some time ago."

"What happened to your plane?"

"What happened to yours?" he countered.

"It burned," said Fred.

The man nodded. "Exactly so."

"And your name? I'm Fred—and that's Lila, and Con, and that's Max."

A look as blank as an iron wall came down over the man's face. "I'm not interested in names. This is the Amazon jungle, not the Travellers Club on Pall Mall."

Con said, "But what do we say, then? I mean, if we need your attention?"

His eyebrows went up so high they nudged at his hairline. "You don't," he said, and he turned away.

He strode across the square, his shoulders hunched, heading toward the place where the vines grew into an impenetrable curtain. He pushed past some branches and disappeared. His footsteps, despite the limp, were astonishingly silent.

"You scared him off!" said Max to Con, his voice full of accusation.

"It wasn't just me! We all did," said Con. "And, technically, I think we *annoyed* him off."

"I didn't know," said Lila, "that asking someone's name would be so controversial."

"I know what we call him," said Max. He beamed up at them proudly. "We call him the explorer."

"But he just said he's not one!" said Con, exasperated. "Weren't you listening?"

"He has an explorer's hat," said Max. "And a vulture. So there."

The Explorer

THE EXPLORER RETURNED AS THEY WERE roasting the caracara, squatting outside their stone room with the meat on sticks. He held a cluster of mangoes balanced along one arm, and a gourd of water in the other hand. They didn't hear him until he was very close. Con jumped, and dropped her hunk of bird in the ashes.

The explorer did not look any of them in the eye. "You're all still growing," he said gruffly. "Especially the small one. It occurred to me the bird might not be enough." He flushed as he set the gourd down next to their fire, dropped the mangoes in Max's lap, and turned on his heel.

Fred jumped to his feet. "Please—just a minute! We wanted to ask—what is this place? Do other people know about it? Do you live alone here?"

"Why? Were you hoping to throw a garden party?"

"I meant, do other people ever come?"

"Sometimes people pass by this place, yes." The explorer squatted down, took Max's meat, which had caught fire, out of his hands, and shook it until it went out. He balanced it in the tips of the flames. "None of them stay long. Some are traveling long distances. Tribespeople. People whose ancestors lived here. They usually stay a few days." He twisted the chunk of bird. Juice dripped from it onto the fire. "But, yes," he said, "in short: People do come."

Con and Lila exchanged delighted glances. Baca, who was unusually full of energy—for a sloth—waved one claw in the air.

"Would they help us?" asked Lila. "Could they take us with them, to Manaus?"

"They might. Very possibly. It depends on the people."

"How often do they come?" asked Fred.

"Oh, every few years." He blew on the meat and handed it to Max. "That's ready."

Fred saw Lila and Con sag. They each looked a little more tired, a little older.

"Years?" said Lila. "Our parents wouldn't be able to wait that long."

"No, I had imagined not," said the explorer.

"But in that case," began Con, "couldn't you—"
She stopped as the vulture flapped out from behind a
stone pillar and came to rest against the man's knee,
eyeing her meat. The bird ruffled its wings and cawed.
Con held her food closer to her chest.

Lila took up her words. "Could you help us get
home?"

The explorer gave them an appraising, sharp-edged
look. "Perhaps."

"Perhaps?" said Lila.

"I could point you toward Manaus. It's a month's
walk, or a week and a half by canoe. I could give you
some provisions. And a map. I might come a short way
with you. I'll have to see."

Lila's eyes lit up. "That would be absolutely wonder—"

"But—," said the explorer.

"But?" Fred held his breath.

"You will have to swear never to speak about this
place, never to tell that you saw a city in the jungle.
More than swear—you will have to prove to me that
you will not."

"What?" Fred stared at the explorer, and then out

past him, across at the stone world sprawling green and yellow and gold away from them into the jungle. "Never tell about all this? Why?"

"Or about me. Ever. All of you. Including the little one."

Fred searched the explorer's face for evidence that he might be joking. "But my father will ask where I was!"

Fred had already imagined the conversation they would have: how he would draw for his father the layout of the city; how he would pace out the distance of the city square and memorize the measurements; how his father would squeeze his shoulder and tell him he had done something remarkable. He had imagined his father telephoning his friend from Oxford who worked at the *Times*. He had imagined his father's voice: "Tim? Listen: My son has done something extraordinary."

The man was watching him, and his face was not sympathetic. "It is very likely," he said, "you will have to lie to him."

"But—no, the whole point of explorers is that they tell people about what they've found! That's what explorers do."

"Exactly so. And I am not an explorer. I am a man who happens to be here."

"But people have been talking about a place like this for hundreds of years!" said Fred. "You have to let everyone know that they weren't just stupid old men with mad theories—they were right!"

"Why do I?"

"Because—if this place does exist, it means they weren't fools—it means they were heroes!" It meant, though Fred did not say it, that it was not foolish, not mad, to dream of being an explorer himself.

"Heroes don't exist, boy—they're inventions made up of newsprint and quotable lines and photogenic mustaches." He grunted in disgust. "Can't bear mustaches myself. Grotesquery mouth-eyebrows, I always thought."

"That's not true! Men died looking for something like this! They died wanting to prove to the world it existed!"

"People have died for many things. It is not difficult to die."

"But you're wrong! The world deserves to know!" Fred felt his forehead burning; he knew he must be turning red. But if they told, his name, and Lila's and

Con's and Max's, would be part of history. Their names would be included in the list of great discoveries.

As if he had read his thought, the explorer curled his lip. "And you, perhaps, wish to be the one to tell them?"

Fred's head jerked backward as if the man had flicked boiling water in his face. "It's not that!"

The explorer blinked a slow, contemptuous blink. "Isn't it?"

Fred clenched one fist. "It would be selfish not to tell!"

"Would it?"

For the first time, Fred realized the others were not joining in. Con sat, looking down at her hands. Lila was stroking Baca with unusual intensity. Max was sucking his wrist, his mouth turned down at the corners.

"Fred," said Lila. Her voice was very quiet, and she didn't look at him. "We need to go home."

Con moved closer to him. She whispered hotly in his ear. "You're being ridiculous! Just promise whatever he wants to get us out of here."

"No," said Fred. He edged away from her.

Con's whisper became a hiss. "We can still tell everyone when we get home—how's he going to know? He's hardly going to be getting newspapers out here!"

"No," said Fred out loud. "I'm not promising anything."

The explorer rose, lit red by the flames of the
fire. The light shone on the scars in the crook of his
elbow, and on his knuckles. "I have asked you to per-
form an easy task—to keep your mouths shut. You are
refusing?"

"No!" said Con. "We'll do whatever you want. Fred,
for goodness' sake, just say it!"

"You can't keep it a secret," said Fred. "It's not your
secret to keep."

"Look," said Con to the explorer, "he might not
promise, but we will! Can't you help us, at least? He
can stay here for all I care."

But the explorer's face was growing red at the neck
and white around his nose and mouth, his whole face
crosshatched with anger. "You"—he glanced at Fred—
"are a fame-hungry, thin-brained ignoramus. And
you"—he glared at Con—"would apparently happily
desert your friend. You disgust me, the lot of you!"

"He's not my friend! Not now."

"Quiet!" Keeping his temper did not seem to be the
explorer's specialty. His voice rose to a roar. "I see no
reason to help any of you! Why should I? Good God, if

children had any use, we surely would have discovered it by now."

He turned away. He shoved his fists into his pockets—and then drew something out. "I'd forgotten: I brought you this. I had not expected your response to my request. None of you deserves it."

Max let out a mew and curled up his knees. The explorer dropped the thing on the ground and strode into the dark. He reached the wall they'd fallen down and began to climb it, fast, using both arms and only one leg, the other swinging loosely at his side.

"Fred!" said Con. "You're completely unfair—and you're welcome to die here yourself, but you've got no right to ruin everything for the rest of us."

Max began to sniff and hiccup with the beginnings of tears.

Fred picked up the thing the explorer had dropped. It was a screw of soft leaves, fastened at the top with thick grass. He opened it. Inside was a pinch of salt, mixed with some flakes of dried green something.

"It's seasoning," he said, "for the bird."

"Stop changing the subject!" snapped Con. "Look, you've got to agree. Go and run after him and tell him you've changed your mind."

"I can't."

"Why not? You don't have to actually do it—you just have to say it!"

"I just can't." He thought of his father. He thought of the going back to school, not just *that Peterson boy, the one with no mother*—but a boy who faced down the jungle and discovered a whole world.

"Please, Fred," said Lila. "Please—do what Con says—run after him. Our parents will be so worried. They might die of it." Max's eyes widened and Lila sighed. "I didn't mean it, Max; it's an expression."

"It's too late, anyway," said Fred. "You heard him. He won't help any of us now. He's too angry."

"Because you *made* him too angry!" said Con.

"So did you!" snapped Fred. "You can do whatever you want. I'm not swearing to a lie, all right?"

"What, because you think you're so high and moral?"

Max covered his ears with his hands.

"No! Because I won't, all right? Because it would be lying about the most important thing that's ever happened to me."

"He'd never know! You just want to get your name in the papers!"

"Yes, he would! He would find out, wouldn't he—because people would have to come and try to find it again, to take photographs and do archaeological digs."

"I don't care what happens once I'm home! This whole place can burn!" Con said.

"Stop it!" shouted Lila. Her voice rang through the clearing. They turned to her in surprise. "Shut up, both of you!" Every inch of her body was stiff with anger. "You're both being disgusting. If it's too late, then there's no point in fighting. And if you make Max cry again, I swear I'll punch you both."

Max climbed into Lila's lap and buried his face in Baca's fur.

Fred swallowed. He tried to recatch his temper. He held out the seasoning.

"Do you want some? We might as well eat."

"No. It could be poisonous," said Con.

Fred withdrew his meat from the fire. It was black in patches, and the skin was charred and steaming. He pulled off the skin with his fingers, wincing at the heat, and sprinkled a pinch of the salt and unknown herbs onto the bird.

Defiantly, averting his eyes from Con's glare, he

took a bite. The first taste of it shot through his whole body; it was a flavor that got into your fingertips, hot and rich and wild.

"Not poisonous," he said. "It's good."

"I hope you choke on it," said Con.

Soon it was entirely dark but for the fire and the moon. The flames cast light out into the city square, throwing its corners into strange dusky shapes. Con shivered as a cloud swept past over the moon, lengthening the shadows. Lila hunched over and began to search Baca's fur for ticks, avoiding Fred's eye.

Fred looked toward the curtain of vines. They hung, in the dark, a great green sweep of shadow covering the right corner of the square.

"What do you think's behind there?" he asked. "What do you think he doesn't want us to see?"

"I don't know," said Con, "and I don't care." She had brushed her hair in front of her eyes so nobody could see her face.

"It could be an animal," said Lila. She glanced up, and then away. "A panther. Like in *The Jungle Book*."

"It might be food stores," said Fred.

Max sat up. "Real food?"

"Why would he keep it there?" said Lila.

"I was thinking, there must have been a place for storing food, when this city was alive. And it's where I'd keep stores, somewhere almost invisible." Fred looked around, checking that the explorer was nowhere near. "I think we should go and look."

"Oh, sure, that's a great idea!" said Con. "You've already made him so angry he's going to let us rot here—why not add stealing his food? He could kill you with his bare hands, but I'm sure that doesn't worry you."

"I wouldn't steal! It would be borrowing. And even then, not unless we have to."

"What do you mean, 'have to'?"

"If he won't help us, we might have to find other ways."

"To do what?" said Con.

"To find enough supplies to start the journey to Manaus." Fred gestured around the empty city. "There's not much food here."

Con was growing red. "You do know this is your fault? You said if we followed the map, we'd get home! And then the second you get here, you ruin it!"

"I didn't!" Fred could feel his neck and cheeks

flushing. "I didn't expect the map to lead to a madman with a pet vulture living alone in an ancient city! That's not something any of us predicted!"

"You promised we'd get home!"

"We *will* get home," said Fred, though he was fairly sure he hadn't promised. Who was he to promise anything? But he only said, "I want to know. Aren't you curious?"

"No," said Con. She swiveled on her bottom and turned her back to him. He could see the sharp thinness of her shoulder blades poking out through her blouse.

"He would never find out." If he could find food, Fred thought, then it wouldn't matter what the explorer said or did; they could get back on the raft and go looking for Manaus. If he could find food, then the chill of Con's anger and Lila's disappointment might be swept away.

"Do what you want. I'm not going over there," said Con.

"Lila?" asked Fred. Lila had been watching them argue, her head turning from one to the other, her eyes growing steadily more unhappy. "It's getting dark. He wouldn't see us. Do you want to come?"

Lila hesitated. "I don't know. He trusted us."

"But he doesn't! He clearly doesn't trust us at all. He won't even tell us his name! Please," said Fred. The wall of vines hung like a threat in the corner of the city square. "It's just to look."

Lila looked out across the dark square. "Fine. Okay. I'll come."

"Thank you!" Fred jumped to his feet. "Are you sure, Con?"

"Very, very sure."

"Could you look after Max?" said Lila. "He's not yet figured out how silence works, really."

Con agreed, though without much pleasure. Fred and Lila moved slowly across the square, feeling their way in the half dark. In between the avenue of trees, the ground was smooth, entirely free of weeds and leaves and jungle debris; but on either side, there were piles of stones, two half-ruined circular mud buildings that looked like grain stores, and shoots of growing things springing up everywhere.

"What do you think this was?" Fred asked.

"I don't know. But if this was the city square, then those statues would be their town monuments. Or maybe their gods."

"Like we have lions in Trafalgar Square?" At the thought of them, a gust of longing for home swept over him.

"Yes! Our papa talks about them. And then everyone could live round the sides of the central avenue, or up in the jungle in tree houses—that's how I'd do it, anyway."

"He's crazy to tell us to keep it secret," said Fred. "It's amazing—it's not like anything I've ever seen in my life." He glanced at Lila from the corner of his eye. "He can't keep it all for himself."

Lila didn't reply. She only stared fixedly ahead.

There was the sound of footsteps running behind them. Fred sprang round, but it was Con, with Max in tow.

"We changed our minds," said Con, panting hard. "But we're not talking to you."

"She made me come," said Max. "She saw a shadow and thought it was a snake."

"I didn't, you little rat!"

Lila and Fred exchanged glances. "You'll have to be quiet, Maxie," said Lila.

"I'm always quiet," said Max with dignity. He turned to put his tongue out at his sister, tripped on a stone, and let out a howl loud enough to wake the sleeping birds. "My toe!"

"Shush!" said Lila.

A tree rustled, then stilled abruptly. Con looked around nervously. "Should we go back?"

Fred shook his head. "You can," he said. "I need to see." As they approached the far end of the square, the clouds moved over the moon, sweeping black shadows over the statues' faces. They looked alive.

Behind the statues ran a great mud and stone wall, high over their heads. The left edge of the wall ended in a crumbling ruin, overrun with patches of light-yellow flowers. The right side vanished in a curtain of vines—the vines the explorer had forbidden them from touching.

Fred approached the vines. They rustled. He stepped backward: It might have been the wind, or something living behind them. He tried not to think of snakes.

He reached out and pushed a handful of vines away. Lila joined him. Behind the vines was another, thicker curtain; they seemed braided together like wicker-work, woven so densely, Fred could barely fit a hand through the green mass. He pushed both arms into the vines, elbow deep, and tugged. There was a flash of color amid the green, then the vines fell back.

"I can see something!" he hissed.

"Shh!" said Con.

"What?" asked Lila.

"I don't know—a piece of yellow—I can't see it anymore. We'll have to cut the vines," he said. He took the knife from his pocket.

"No, wait!" said Con. "I don't know if that's a good idea."

"It is," said a voice over their heads, "an exceptionally bad idea."

Fred froze. There was the smack of shoe on stone, and the explorer jumped down from the top of the wall, landing inches in front of Fred's face, grunting as his bad leg hit the ground. He straightened up, his face rigid with fury.

"I asked you to *stay away*," he said softly. "Is that so difficult?"

A cold dread shot through Fred; the look on the explorer's face was worse than being caned at school. "I'm—really sorry." Fred's tongue was suddenly dry. "We just thought—"

"You *thought*. Are you so grotesquely lacking in

self-control that you cannot let a single idle thought pass through your minds without acting on it?"

"We're so sorry—," began Lila.

"Just get away from here!" said the explorer. His skin radiated hot rage.

Desperation was rising in Fred's blood; he could see Max shaking with fear. He stepped in front of him. "We weren't going to take anything," he said. He felt the burn of the lie flood through him, and stumbled over the words. "We just needed to see—"

"I said go! Just go!"

"It was my fault," said Fred. "It was my idea, not theirs—"

"I don't care whose idea it was." The explorer pulled the knife from his belt. He pointed it at Fred's chest. "Go to bed. If I *ever* find you anywhere near the vines again, I'll cut off your fingers while you sleep and fry them in banana oil and feed them to the vulture for dessert."

Fred turned and led the way back down the center of the boulevard, shame pulsing in his chest. Even Max didn't make a sound.

The Trap

FRED WOKE TWICE IN THE NIGHT TO FIND his nose pressed against the bare stones and mud of the floor and his breath coming in gasps. His father's back was turned to him, and he would not look around, even though Fred screamed until his lungs were empty.

"A dream," he muttered. "Dreams don't matter. Not real." But it had felt very real; real like blood is real.

Fred looked up through the vines to the canopy above them; he squinted, trying to memorize every inch. The second he got home, he would draw the canopy for his father, in full color. His father would buy him pencils in a dozen different greens.

Fred did not want to risk closing his eyes again. It was a powerful relief when the sun came up and he could creep out of the stone hut into its warmth.

There was a chilly lump of guilt sitting in his stomach, left over from the night before. He had never stolen anything in his life, never even tried. He looked toward the vines, shining vivid emerald in the morning light. He thought of the look on the explorer's face. It had been more than angry; it had had fear in it.

He would have to apologize. The thought made Fred's stomach squirm with humiliation, but he could not leave the explorer thinking he was a habitual thief, a liar, a cheat. He wasn't sure if the man was the kind to accept apologies; it might be akin to apologizing to one of the stone statues. But he would try.

He tipped up his boots, checking them for scorpions; all the books he'd read had been very urgent on the matter of scorpions.

Fred's fingers were clumsier than usual; his whole upper body was quivering with nerves.

The ruin looked different in the sunrise. It looked more alive. There were places where vines had covered the half-fallen remnants of walls that ran along the far end of the square; places, too, where the vines had been hacked back and he could see the marks on the stone where it had been cut from the parent rock.

Fred walked slowly through the open square,

staring upward. The canopy over them was intricately constructed, woven from the branches rising from the trees that had sprouted among the stones and nestled against the city walls, and from a network of vines. It was a green tablecloth for a giant laid out atop the trees.

There were holes in the green scattered everywhere, where the sun burst through in bright light, and one vast gap, just above the statues, where the stones shone yellow. Directly under it, a single tree stood, burned of all leaves. Perhaps by the sun, Fred thought, or a very small forest fire.

A tiny mouselike creature with enormous ears was basking in the heat of the morning; it scuttled away as he came near.

Fred approached the stone statues, his stomach knotting tighter with every step. They were twice as tall as he was, and so worn by rain and time that their faces were smoothed of expression—the man and the woman were identifiable only by their bodies, the panther by her tail—but still, in places, he could see where tools had cut at the stone. He reached out and touched the paw of the panther. Only half of it remained, but he could see where her claws would have been, how her yellow stone would have glowed when she was new.

The explorer, though, was nowhere to be seen.

Fred was just about to turn tail and run when he heard deep breathing ahead of him.

A tree had grown up through the stone floor to the left side of the statues. The explorer was asleep in a hammock woven from lianas, in the shade of the tree. He lay in it diagonally; stretched out in that direction it was almost as flat as a bed. Fred made a mental note to only lie in hammocks diagonally from now on.

Under the hammock was a cluster of things: a small pot of ink, a quill made from a vulture feather, a piece of bark with some notes, and an enormous pair of shoes.

Fred moved closer. The explorer looked much younger asleep, and softer.

"Boy." The man did not open his eyes; at least, he didn't seem to. "I hope you have a good reason for waking me."

Fred's chest grew hot. "Sorry, I—," he began. How had he known it was him? He must, Fred thought, have been peeping from between his eyelashes.

"I could smell you," said the explorer, as if Fred had asked the question aloud. "And you all breathe differently. The English girl breathes through her teeth, the Brazilian girl with the rope of hair breathes as though she fears waking the world. The small boy appears to be breathing through a veritable revolutionary barricade of snot. And right now, you are breathing as if you are afraid I plan to throw a knife into your kneecap."

Fred flinched, but the explorer did not seem to notice; he sighed and stretched.

"It's no good. I'm awake now."

"Oh. I hope you slept well?" asked Fred.

The explorer sat up and scratched his chin. "This isn't a rooming house in Bournemouth. You don't have to talk like an old woman."

Fred felt his forehead grow hot. "I was trying to be polite. My father says, 'Be ruthlessly polite, if only because it's easier than all the alternatives.'"

"How practical of him." The explorer extracted a red and black beelike insect from the hem of his trouser leg and crushed it between his palms. "In future, boy, it's best not to come near me when I'm sleeping. If you need to wake me, throw something from a safe distance."

"Why?"

"I have a startle reflex." Fred must have looked as

puzzled as he felt, because the man added, "I was captured once."

"By Germans?"

"No."

"By natives?"

"Not by the people you're thinking of—not by the indigenous people to whom this land belongs, no. By the owners of a rubber company. I didn't like how they were treating the people who lived in the forests around them."

"Is that how your leg—"

"I have very little desire to talk about it."

Fred stepped backward. There are looks that make you want to hide behind your own back. He forced himself to speak: "I wanted to come and say, I'm really sorry. About last night." It was coming out wrong—he sounded as if he were apologizing for failing to hold open a door. He swallowed. "Properly sorry."

The explorer raised a single, unimpressed eyebrow.

Fred began to stammer. Fear dug into his belly. "It wasn't—we weren't going to do anything; we're weren't going to take anything, or break anything. But—"

"But it was dishonest and counterproductive?" said the explorer drily. "Quite."

Fred flushed. For the first time, he met the explorer's eye. He nodded. "Yes. It was. I didn't mean to be those things. But I was. You're right to be angry." He stared at the floor as he turned away, back toward the sleeping house.

"Wait."

Fred turned. The explorer began to tie his shoes, meticulously tugging at the ends of the laces to get them exactly even. Then he pulled a knife from his pocket and began to sharpen the blade on a rock. Fred waited, the tension building in his chest. He wondered if the man really was planning to cut off his fingers. He thrust his hands deep in his pockets.

At last the explorer said, "I'm going to set a trap." He splashed water on his face. "You might as well learn how if you're going to provide for yourselves on your trek home." Carefully, methodically, the man began to shave with the knife. "You interested in coming?"

"Yes!" said Fred. "Very."

"Just a moment then." The man puckered his mouth, pulling the skin on his cheek taut. "I warn you—you can't let a beard grow too long out here. Next thing you know you've a family of glowworms living in your sideburns." He looked sternly at Fred. "Which is not as appealing as it sounds."

"Thank you," said Fred. He tried not to laugh. "I'll remember that. Although I can't actually grow a beard."

The explorer pulled off his jacket and hooked it on a branch on the tree. The jacket was made from a variety of dark furs; some still had legs attached. The tree, Fred could see, was used as a kind of wardrobe; it also held a spare shirt, hanging from a convenient branch.

Fred looked closer. The branch the coat hung on had been tied on by hand, looped in a figure eight with vines. He felt a jag of recognition run through his blood. He shivered.

The explorer looked surprised. "Are you unwell, boy?"

"No! Nothing like that. It's just—I've seen a branch tied on like that before. On a mooring post. At the den. Near the bees. It must have been you."

"Very likely. I use that knot a good deal. It lasts for years if you get it right. Are you sure you're not sick?" The explorer looked sharply at him. "I have no wish to care for a sick child. There's a waterproof greatcoat I made somewhere, if you don't mind the smell of fish."

"I'm fine, really."

"And I made a scarf once, out of monkeys."

"Monkeys?" Fred tried not to look as appalled as he felt.

"Yes. But they kept fighting and it wasn't worth the fleas."

"You made a scarf out of *alive* monkeys?"

"A scarf may have been a somewhat hubristic exaggeration—I draped half a dozen small monkeys around my shoulders. It was not ideal." The explorer set off up the steep incline that surrounded the clearing. "Keep up."

"Were they tame?"

"I thought they were." He picked up a machete, smacked the flat side against his palm. "I'd been taming them for a year. It turned out they were less docile than I imagined. Until you've had a monkey mistake your nose for a fig, you don't know what waking up too suddenly means." The explorer strode out, heading to where the forest grew thickly.

"Don't lag!" he called. Fred thought guiltily about the others, who might at any moment wake up and find him gone, but most of his energy was needed to keep up with the man's pace. Despite his limp, he moved twice as fast as Fred, and five times as quietly.

"Don't we need to mark the trees to find our way back?" panted Fred.

The explorer turned. He looked astonished, or it might, Fred thought, have been affront.

"What do you take me for? No, we don't need to mark the trees, no more than you would need to mark the wall between your bedroom and your lavatory. This is my home."

He gestured to the trees around them, which were thinner than those circling the city, and a lighter shade of green.

"We'll get wood here, for the trap. See this?" He pointed to a branch as thick as Fred's wrist.

"Cut me two branches like that. They should be as straight as possible. That's a good tree over there. Here." He handed Fred the machete and began stripping down a vine into a thin rope.

The machete had a wonderful weight to it; it was exquisitely made, with a carved handle and a blade that caught the sun and threw back light in silver and green.

"This is beautiful," said Fred. He gave it an experimental swipe.

"Watch it! Kindly refrain from chopping off your

own hand. And cut straight, boy! Don't damage the trees." The explorer bent and brushed some debris away from a green shoot so pale it was almost white. "And cut only what you need. Don't hoard. Leave enough that the tree can replenish itself. The greatest threat to living things is man, which is not a thought to make one proud." He waved a hand to encompass the close-growing trees, the boundless green spreading leaves. "It is humans who bring about the end of all this. Do you understand? The city, and the trees that disguise it from the land and sky? It needs protecting."

"Protecting from us, though?" said Fred. He swept the machete through the air again; it made a very satisfying whistling sound. "What could we do to it?"

"You can *talk*. Children are terrible at keeping secrets. And some kinds of knowledge are vulnerable, like a breathing thing; they require great care."

"I've kept hundreds of secrets!" Fred said. But as he turned toward the trees, he wondered if that was true. He had never had a secret so valuable. He had never had a secret that would make his father put down his newspaper and turn to look at him.

"This place needs protecting from humans," said the explorer. "I find it hard not to be wary of my fellow countrymen. They care about the wrong things. I used to sit in the train carriage with the same men every day, on the seven fifteen to Paddington—and I would look at them and think: You wake up in the morning and you put on your trousers and you don't even think about the beauty of the Amazon River! How do you justify that?

"And I did not admire our prime minister. He is very well dressed, but despite his many protestations to the contrary, I am not one hundred percent convinced he can read."

He shot out a sudden hand and grabbed Fred's wrist, mid–machete swipe.

"Boy! Careful—hold it with the blade facing away from you. Cutting yourself with a machete is extremely gauche. Here—cut that branch—the green one."

Fred swept the machete down over a branch as thick as his wrist. The first time, the machete got stuck in the wood and he tugged at it.

"I recommend you take care," said the explorer. "Whatever our differences of opinion, I have no wish to see you open a blood vessel."

On the second try, the branch came away with a satisfying thump.

"Good. Are you watching? I do not expect to have to show you twice."

The explorer selected a springy sapling tree, four feet tall, its trunk barely thicker than Fred's thumb. "Tie the rope around the tip of the sapling," he said.

Fred did so while the explorer searched around the ground and located a Y-shaped branch, the size and shape of a slingshot. "Good. Hand me the machete." He held out his hand, a surgeon midoperation. Carefully, using the handle of the machete, he knocked the Y-shaped branch into the ground near the sapling, so that only the Y was showing.

"Now, tie the other end of the rope around your green branch—in the middle, yes—but leave the end free. The end needs to be a noose—a loop knot. We are building a spring snare."

Fumbling, Fred followed the man's instructions. He had practiced knot tying in his bedroom, under the covers late at night, in the forbidden small hours. The explorer nodded approval, and Fred felt a surge of pride prickle in his fingers.

"Now watch." The man pulled down on the rope, and the sapling bent forward as if saluting. He wedged the green branch into the Y, the rope stretched taut.

"The slightest movement will make the green branch spring free. So an animal puts its foot in the noose, the sapling springs up, the slipknot tightens—and you have dinner."

"What's it for?" Fred asked, examining it from every angle. "What does it catch?"

"Come on," said the explorer. "Let's go. I have other things to do. It's for whatever crawls into it. Rats, armadillos."

"You eat rats?"

"Of course. If I have to. I've eaten many things over the years that I have not precisely enjoyed but have appreciated nonetheless. Snails, spiders."

"Spiders?"

"Certain spiders are remarkably delicious. I could help you find them. But I have no desire to help you unless you swear to keep silent about this place."

Fred bit his lips together.

"No?" the explorer said. "You would prefer to align yourself with men who loot from the land and its history?"

"They don't!" Fred thought of the men striding across the pages of his books. "They don't all do that!"

"Certainly, there are some who do not, but how

many? You wish to invite the world to come and stare; you gamble on the morality of the world at large, do you?"

Fred's stomach contracted. He said nothing. His heart thrummed painfully, but he forced himself not to look away.

Brusquely, the explorer took the machete from Fred and began to hack off thick branches for firewood. His ring caught the light.

Fred tried to change the subject. "Your ring." He was about to say, *Why do you wear a ring in the jungle?* but, he thought, the explorer didn't seem to welcome personal questions; and he was swinging the machete very close to Fred's knees. "Um . . . what's it made from?"

"Snake scales, and caiman bone." The explorer's pride in it seemed to wrestle with his anger at Fred; then he took the ring off and held it out. "Here." On the inside rim, words had been cut.

Fred read: "*Nec . . . Aspera Terrent?*"

"Latin. Roughly, it means, 'Difficulties be damned.' Do you think it's peculiar, to wear a ring out here?"

Fred did think exactly that, but it seemed a bad place and time to say so. He laughed awkwardly instead.

The explorer raised his eyebrows. "While we're on the subject—why did you dress like a minor state administrator to come to the jungle? You look like you're running for mayor of Tunbridge Wells."

Fred looked down at himself in surprise. "This is—was—my school uniform. My father says you should always wear a uniform where possible. He's that kind of man. I didn't know I was coming to the jungle."

"You should always dress as if you *might* be going to the jungle. You never know when you might meet an adventure."

"I'm at a boarding school. In Norfolk. Gresham's. On the Cromer Road."

"And?"

"It's just, I'm much more likely to meet a geography teacher than an adventure."

The explorer looked at the world around them, and then, hard, at Fred. "And yet, here you are," he said.

Carefully he detached a branch covered in berries from a tree and threw it to Fred, who caught it, realizing a second too late that the branch was covered in thorns. He said some words his school did not allow him to say.

The explorer arched his left eyebrow a quarter of an inch. Fred instantly stopped swearing.

"Make sure the small one—the boy with the leaking nose—eats some. He's too thin. Try one."

Fred put the largest berry in his mouth. The juice burst on his tongue; it was absolutely hideous. He wanted to spit it out, but he had a feeling the explorer would not approve; he swallowed, and scrubbed his tongue on the back of his hand. "It tastes of gasoline!" he said. "And badgers."

"I know. But you should eat them anyway; they're rich in vitamins. And they'll be easy to find on your road to Manaus; they grow near the river."

"I think maybe I'd rather starve."

"No, you wouldn't. It's a long walk. It's best not to get too hungry if you can avoid it. If you get hungry enough, you will start feeling that your bad ideas are your good ones. If you get truly famished, you'll start feeling like a French philosopher, and that's unwise."

And he strode back through the trees, leaving Fred to run, jumping over roots and anthills to keep pace with him.

Tarantulas

Y THE TIME FRED GOT BACK, THE OTHERS
were awake, and furious, and eating.

It is difficult to look angry and chew at the
same time, so they put down their bananas to glare at
him.

"Where were you?" asked Lila.

"We thought he might have been cutting off your
fingers," said Con.

Fred explained, about the trap, about the statues,
and proffered the berries as a peace offering.

By the time they'd finished spitting out the berries,
and Max had finished miming being sick on Fred's
shoes, Con and Lila had stopped glaring quite so ferociously.

Lila offered him three quarters of a banana.

"We found them over there—there's a tree, behind

that cluster of stones—where the earth shows through. There were five, but we took only three, in case they belong to"—she gestured with her head, up toward the statues— "*him.*"

The banana was a little green, but Fred preferred them that way. He ate as slowly as he could, but it was difficult; bananas were very rare at home. It tasted of comfort.

A light thumping echoed across the city square; it was the explorer stomping down the center of the citadel, heading in their direction.

They began frantically tidying themselves—Con raking her hair with her fingers, Lila straightening Baca's fur. Max licked his forearms like a cat.

At that point, several things happened at once. The explorer came closer. He didn't, in fact, seem to be looking at them. He seemed lost in thought, staring upward at the canopy as he walked.

A rustling made Fred look away, down at the ground.

And a snake reared up from behind a fallen branch. It stood straight up, like the periscope on a submarine. It was violent green, with a whitish belly. Its eyes were red. Fred gave a hiss, and gestured to the others. They froze.

"Don't panic," whispered Lila. "Snakes don't attack, remember?"

Fred backed away. The snake came up over the trunk, its neck still a stalk, heading toward him. It didn't seem to like him staring.

"I think the snake might not know that," whispered Fred.

The snake started to glide across the log toward them. Fred's breath halted in the middle of his throat. He looked around wildly for a stick.

The explorer walked straight past them, chewing on a stick with fierce intent. Without pausing in his stride, without seeming to take aim, he pulled a rock from his pocket and threw it at the snake. It cut through the air and struck the snake in the neck. The snake slumped to the ground.

The explorer kept walking. He didn't look back. His eyes returned to the canopy overhead.

Fred stared at Lila, at Con, and saw his own shock reflected back twice over.

"Where did he learn to do that?" whispered Lila.

"And *why*?" hissed Con. "I thought he'd rather we were all dead—it'd be more convenient for him."

"Don't you say that!" said Max. "You can't!" His face

was full of righteous fury. "He killed the snake for us! And he's *mine*!"

The explorer stopped walking, and his head whipped round to look at them. Con's mouth snapped shut, and she backed behind Fred, but the man's eyes were on Max.

The explorer strode back toward them. He bent, picked up the limp body of the snake, and thrust it into his pocket.

His voice was abrupt, and without gentleness. "I have no wish to have it on my conscience if you die. Have none of you any idea what to do if you see a snake?"

"No," said Fred. That should have been fairly clear, he thought.

The explorer sighed. "For future reference: Walk away, backward, as fast as you can. Don't run. And hum as you go."

"You want us to serenade a snake?" said Con. "Why?"

"They don't like the vibration. Or, if you can kill it, it makes a reasonable dinner. If you really plan to make the journey to Manaus, you should know that. There are a great many things you need to know how to do. Can you fish?"

"No," said Fred. "Not really."

"Can you hunt?"

"No," said Lila.

"Can you set traps? Any of you except Fred, who should now know?"

"No," said Con. "Why would we be able to? I live with a great-aunt. She doesn't trap anything except dust. And mice. But she doesn't eat them." Lila grinned at her, her wonky tooth shining conspiratorially.

"I see." The explorer drew in breath, a heave of air that seemed to cement a decision. "Right then. Come with me."

"Just Con," said Lila, "or all of us?"

"All of you. Even Fred, despite his idiocy." His eyes were hard. "Even the miniature cataclysm in the cardigan."

"He means you, Max," said Con.

"I've found a nest," said the explorer. "And I will share it with you. But I want to be clear—this is the only help I will give you. I have no time to waste on children."

"A nest of what?" said Lila. She scooped Baca up and settled him in her arms. He grasped hold of her upper arm and rested his nose in the crook of her elbow.

"You'll see."

You'll see, Fred thought as they marched in single file behind the explorer, half running to keep up. "You'll see" were not reassuring words when spoken by someone whose fur coat still has the feet and faces attached.

The nest, when they reached it, sticky with sweat and their hair full of twigs, did not look as Fred had expected. It was a hole in the ground. In fact, it was barely even that; the ground was covered in dry leaves, and the hole was almost invisible.

"What's in there?" asked Fred. He wondered if it might be mice. Did mice dig burrows? He wasn't sure how he would feel about eating a mouse.

"Tarantulas," said the explorer.

"Oh." Mice suddenly sounded much more appetizing, thought Fred.

"They're delicious. They taste like shrimp cocktail." The explorer looked at Con, whose mouth was open. "Do you have a plan for your face, or are you going to keep it like that?"

"You don't actually eat tarantulas?" asked Con.

"Do they attack sloths?" asked Lila. Baca peered out from her elbow.

"We get to eat spiders!" said Max.

The three sentences were spoken very differently, Fred thought: disgust, cautious interest, sheer unholy joy. He said nothing, only knelt down to stare more closely at the hole.

"Yes. You toast them over the fire, like crumpets."

"But aren't they poisonous?" asked Lila.

"I am not eating a tarantula," said Con.

"As you wish." The explorer shrugged. "If you plan to walk to Manaus, the day will come when you'll be glad of knowing how. Right. We'll need some long twigs."

"I'm not eating one," said Con. "That shouldn't be a shocking position to take!" She turned to Lila and Fred for confirmation. "That's normal!"

"I want to try it," said Fred.

"Why on earth?"

"Because I don't want us to starve on the walk to Manaus. And what else are we going to eat? And what if it's good?"

Lila's face was interested. "What do you think are the chances it will be? Percentage-wise?"

"Low," said Con. "Really, disgustingly low."

"Who wants to go first?" asked the explorer. There was a glimmer in his eyes. Fred didn't absolutely trust him.

Fred looked down at the hole; he thought he saw a

shadow move inside it. His stomach rumbled. "I will," he said.

"Fine." The explorer smiled; it was not an easy smile. There was something wolfish about it. "It's very simple—take a stick and jab it in the hole. The tarantula will come out to see what's happening."

Fred crouched over the hole, and shook the tip of his stick backward and forward over the tarantula nest.

"You have officially crossed the line between brave and a medical condition," said Con.

"It can take a while, so don't give up," said the explorer. "It's a good season for tarantulas. They should be meaty."

"He's mad," whispered Con to Lila. "We're alone in a jungle with an actual, real-life madman."

Fred kept shaking his stick. Nothing happened. Con visibly relaxed.

"It's empty!" she said. "Thank goodness, it's empty!"

Four legs, jointed, thin, and hairy, emerged from the nest. Fred froze.

"Keep going!" barked the explorer. "Move the stick backward! Lure it out!"

The spider that emerged was as big as Fred's palm, and light brown.

"It's a female," said the explorer. "The males are black." His hand darted past Fred and he grasped hold of the tarantula around the middle. He held his fingers well back from the pincers, which waved, irately, at the air.

"Do you want to stroke it?" he asked.

Sloths, when anxious, make noises halfway between a sheep and a seagull. Baca let out a tiny, shrill bleat. Lila stepped back, her arm shielding the sloth's eyes.

The honest answer, Fred thought, was no. It was a *no* loud enough to shake the foundations of the jungle. But the words that came out of his mouth were, "Which way do I stroke it?"

"In the direction of the fur—from the head to the back end."

"Don't, Fred!" said Con. She was standing with her back flat against a tree. She was pale under the dirt. "He's angry at you, remember! He's trying to hurt you!"

The explorer's voice was dangerously mild. "The bite of this species is no worse than a bee sting," he said. He held the tarantula very gently. "My boy used to—" And then he stopped, shook himself, and said,

"I knew of a child, once, who had one as a pet. It got tame enough to sit in his lap while he ate."

Fred glanced at the explorer, but his face was impassive. He laid his finger on the tarantula. It was unexpectedly soft. It quivered under his touch.

"Now," said the explorer, pulling a knife from his pocket, suddenly very brisk, "you slice along the back, from the neck—here, so it feels no pain, like this—but don't cut the head off," and he cut across the spider's neck, "and wrap it in leaves." He dropped the spider onto a large leaf and handed it to Lila, who shuddered, but held it in both hands.

"Now you tie it with grass, as if it were a parcel—yes, good. There's another nest, east of here. Remember, you can tell a tarantula hole from the opening: shallow at the front, and then a sudden dip into a tunnel. The journey to Manaus takes you through rocky terrain; you'll be able to find them there quite easily. I once went a whole month eating nothing but spiders and bananas. I had terrible yellow diarrhea, but I survived."

He set off through the jungle without glancing behind him. Fred looked down at his hands. They smelled very slightly acidic.

By the time they caught up to him, the explorer was leaning over another hole, sweeping back leaves and plants with his caiman-skin shoe. This hole was significantly larger.

"Now, the tarantula you have wrapped up like a birthday present is a common tarantula. But this hole"—he prodded it with a stick—"is different. This is the hole of a Goliath tarantula: *Theraphosa blondi.*" He glanced pointedly at Con's hair. "The Goliath tarantula has hairs on its rump, which it sheds if it feels threatened. And God knows I'd feel threatened if faced with a bunch of children. The hairs sting if they get on your skin, like nettles but far worse. Do you understand?"

"Yes."

"Good. Never mix up your tarantulas if you're planning to stroke them."

It seemed sensible advice, Fred thought, if useful only in very rare circumstances.

"Are they the ones they call birdeaters?" asked Lila.

"Exactly," said the explorer, looking down with something like approval. "Although they rarely eat birds. Mostly toads, and worms, and the occasional rat."

They did not need to tempt out the Goliath tarantula; as Fred leaned forward to peer into the hole, the front legs emerged. He stepped backward, fast.

Four more legs followed, and a great round body, covered in thick hair. Con retched. Max squealed with delight. Lila stepped in front of her brother, pushing him behind her. She clutched Baca more tightly.

The spider was as big as Max's face. It moved slowly, toward Max's ankles.

As calmly as if he were tying a shoelace, the explorer reached down, pressed the spider to the ground with a stick, and gathered up the legs in his fingers. "Hand me some leaves, one of you. And watch your feet! There'll be more."

By late afternoon they had six tarantulas. They took them home to their fire, and Lila laid them neatly in a row.

"Good. Now, you toast them on sticks until all the hair burns off," said the explorer. "They'll start giving off a squeaking noise; that's the hot air escaping from the space between the leg joints. That's a sign they're done. You can eat all of it, including the face."

"The face," said Con weakly.

The explorer laughed. He picked up two of the parcels, leaving them four. "You're on your own now," he said. "Don't disturb me again, or I'll serve your

eyeballs to the caiman like olives at a cocktail party."
They stared at the great bulk of his retreating back as
he strode into the jungle.

Fred speared his tarantula on a stick and held it over
the fire, watching it turn dark brown in the flames.
Lila toasted Max's for him. Con's lay still in its parcel.
She refused to look at it.

"It's a *spider*," she kept whispering.

After ten minutes the spiders began to whistle, a
sound like a teakettle.

Fred gathered all his courage together. He pulled
the tarantula off the stick: It was hot and crispy, but it
looked unambiguously spidery. He held his nose, and
bit a leg off.

He was astonished. They tasted a little fishlike, and
salty, like the sea. He took another, larger bite. "It's not
bad!" he said.

Con stared at him, incredulous. "You're eating spiders, you do realize that?"

Max took a bite of his. "It's *very* delicious," he said.
"Can I eat yours, if you're not having it?"

"No," said Con.

"Try a leg of mine," said Fred. The spider made
him feel more awake. He could imagine the journey

home—really imagine it—for the first time: walking by day and eating spiders and whatever fruit they could find each night. He thought of his father meeting him at the dock in Portsmouth, bending to pull Fred into his arms. He shook himself and tried to push the thought away.

"It tastes of fishy chicken," said Lila. "Really, truly, it's not bad."

"Promise it's not a trick?"

"Promise. Try mine. Fred burned his." Lila held out a spider leg.

Very gingerly, Con took the leg from Lila. She sniffed it. "It doesn't smell of anything—just the fire," she said suspiciously. She closed her eyes and bit the tip off the foot. Her eyes opened in surprise. "It's . . . not terrible!" she said. "It tastes almost like food."

"I love them." Max spoke with half a spider leg hanging out of his mouth. "They should sell them at the circus, with the ice cream."

Twice-Fried _Oiseau Spectacle_

AS EVENING FELL, FRED AND LILA AND CON formed a conclave. They sat in a tight circle around their fire, their heads close together, planning in whispers. Max lay on his back on the stones and decorated himself with the small cloverlike plants growing at his feet. Baca sat on Lila's lap, watching with careful eyes.

"I think we should cook something for him," said Lila, gesturing with her chin up toward the statues and the vines. "Then he might help us again."

"Yes!" said Con. "Men love food."

"No! I don't want him to take my ears!" said Max.

"He was joking, Max," said Lila.

"We hope," muttered Con, but for once she said it under her breath.

"That sounds great—but we can't really cook," said Fred.

"You don't get to have an opinion," said Con haughtily. "If it weren't for you, we wouldn't have to worry about him. Anyway, good cooking is simply paying attention and taking your time." She spoke as if reciting.

"I like that! Who told you that?" asked Lila.

"Well. My gym teacher."

"Are gym teachers famous for being good cooks?" asked Fred. He scratched a mosquito bite and winced; it had begun to bleed.

"No. She was a terrible gym teacher. She made us walk around the gym pretending to be riding a horse. She said it would be good for our self-confidence."

"Was it?"

"What do you think?"

Lila grinned. "We still have those berries," she said. "We could roast them for him. With some of the left-over bird."

They looked at the bird. It had dried out a little in the sun. "It smells very, very leftover," said Con.

"At home," said Lila, "we have refried beans from the

day before. Mama makes them with spices. It's delicious."

Her smile faded a little at the word "mama." Con looked for a long second at Lila, then got briskly to her feet. "I'll find a stone we can use as a frying pan," she said.

"We could call it twice-fried bird spectacular," said Lila.

"Twice-fried *oiseau spectacle*," said Con. "That's French. Posh food is always in French."

A sudden sound made them stop talking. From the far side of the square, in among the vines, came a roaring. It sounded like a bear, or a tiger, or an engine, or a human in pain.

Lila reached for Baca on her shoulder. "Is that . . . him?"

The sound stopped as suddenly as it had begun. "Maybe . . . he goes there to scream? To roar? Maybe that's what he's doing?" asked Con. "I'd quite like a room I could scream in."

They sat in silence for many minutes, but the noise didn't come again. They returned to the food. The vulture approached. He sat on Max's shoe and watched balefully as they cooked, apparently resenting that they had not offered him any.

"I didn't know vultures could look so much like aunts," said Con.

When the explorer finally reappeared, though, he seemed to have forgotten that they were there. He looked briefly startled, then he nodded at them, as if to commuters sharing a train, and was turning away without a word when Max ran after him, weaving in and out of the young shoots growing up between the stones of the city floor.

"Come back!" said Max. It was an order, not a request. "We cooked you food!"

The explorer looked surprised. "What? Oh, that's very generous, but I won't, thank you."

"You have to! We made it specially."

The explorer crouched down in front of Max. "I applaud your decision to move commandingly through the world, but you have vulture poo in your hair, which dents your gravitas."

"Please?" said Lila. She had moved silently across the square, approaching him as you would a wild animal. Baca looked out at the world through Lila's hair. "Please just try it?"

She held out a leaf, on which was laid some of the bird and some roasted berries. They had tried to make it look as much like a restaurant plate as possible. Due to an accident involving the vulture and Max's elbow, the meat was more covered in ash than any of them had planned, but, Fred thought, you could still make out what it was supposed to be.

"It's twice-fried wazoo," said Max. "It's special."

"Well. Thank you," said the explorer. He took a bite. Then he gave an exclamation and spat it into a bush. "Good heavens! That tastes like being punched in a graveyard."

"Oh. Sorry," said Lila, her voice very small. "We wanted to do something that you'd like, so we—"

"Please don't cut off our ears," said Max.

"No—I apologize. It was a kind thought." The explorer touched the ring on his little finger. "I had rather forgotten how kind children can be." Then he shook his head so hard that his shock of hair flicked sweat onto the stones, and turned, giving a half bow. "You'll forgive me: I must light a fire before dark."

He paced to the far side of the square, close to his hammock, and knelt among branches. It took him less than a minute to have the flames sparking from the wood; he moved so fast and with so much assurance that it was impossible to follow his hands. He took a fish from his pocket and set it on a three-cornered spit. The vulture kept close to his ankles.

He sank down and squatted by the fire. Fred watched from a corner of his eye while the others grimly attempted to chew the twice-burnt bird. The explorer sat, his elbows on his knees, staring at nothing.

"Do you think he's all right?" Fred whispered. "He looks—I don't know—sad."

Con looked over. "He kills snakes with rocks. That sort of person doesn't get sad."

As they spoke, the explorer rose and crossed to a pile of coconuts at the foot of a tree. Each had been sliced open at the top and then had the lid replaced, attached on a swivel with a spike. The explorer drank deeply from one, threw away the shell, and picked up another. After his third, he turned suddenly to the children.

"Do you drink?" he called across the clearing.

"It depends what sort of drinking," called back Con.

"Cachaça, my own version. Try some."

They crossed the square warily, keeping a close eye on the vulture. Lila slipped Baca down the front of her sweater and laid a protective hand on his head, and the other on Max's shoulder.

They hovered, the four of them, on the edge of the

light cast by the fire. Fred bent his knees to sit, but none of the others did, so he tried to make it look as if he were testing his joints.

"Sit down, boy!" said the explorer. "All of you. Do you not know what God gave you arses for? Here—drink this."

"What is it?" said Fred.

"Sugarcane. Coconut milk. And some other things. Herbs."

"What kind of herbs?" asked Lila.

"Have you ever drunk anything that tastes like it will either kill you or make you immortal? That's this."

Fred took a mouthful, and doubled over, coughing. It tasted of nothing, really, only hot, and burning. It made his nose and eyes stream.

"More?" said the explorer.

"No, thank you. It tastes too much like being electrocuted."

The explorer laughed. The laugh had thorns in it. "You'll like it better when you're older."

Con sniffed the liquid. "Is it alcohol?"

The explorer shrugged. "Technically, yes, but not the way you're thinking. It doesn't taste like wine or have the same effect."

Con shook her head. Lila, to Fred's surprise, reached for the coconut. "Just so I know. If I want to be a scientist, I need to experiment."

She drank. Baca tried to drink too, and had to have his upper body fished out of the coconut. Lila shook her head vehemently. "It tastes like puking, the wrong way around."

The explorer grunted. "Ungrateful baggage."

He took the fish from the spike, laid it on a stone, sliced it down the middle, and cut out four chunks from its flesh.

"Eat this. Better than that horrendous nightmare of a bird you concocted."

The fish was hot and rich; it was unexpectedly meaty in flavor, smoky and bold. Fred ate his in two bites, and looked hopefully at what was left.

"Piranha," said the explorer. "The older they are when you catch them, the more they taste like chicken."

The explorer seemed surprisingly disposed to talk. He made a sweeping gesture with his hand, hit the vulture in the chest, and sloshed some of the coconut's liquid over the bird.

"Tell me—what do you think of this?"

"The vulture?" said Con doubtfully. Her voice took

on the tone that voices take when asked to comment on a newborn baby when that baby is self-evidently horrifyingly ugly. "It's . . . nice. It smells very . . . original."

"Of the city! Of the jungle! They call it the green hell. Did you know that?"

Fred stared at the vast expanse of stone, at the green ceiling high, high overhead.

"They call the jungle the green hell because it is lacking in grand pianos. Men—and when I say 'men,' I mean idiots—used to come out here with pianos on the backs of elephants. And they used to be angry when their teacups broke in the storms." He grunted. "But if you're willing to have a roughish, wildish kind of life—I find it closer to heaven than to hell."

The explorer began to drink from another coconut shell. He sighed, and his eyes became misty. "There's a lot written about love at first sight. And what is love at first sight but recognition? It's instant knowledge: that this is a person who will make your heart larger—a lover, a child. The same applies to places. It's why I wanted to seek them out. It's why they need protecting."

The explorer stared, his eyelids a little uneven, at Fred.

Fred stared at the fire, avoiding his gaze. There

was a quality in this place that worked like flint on his insides: It was the light, and the vastness of it, and the sun, and the green. He could see why other people might feel it was too green, too loud, too endless, too *much*; but for him, it felt like a trumpet call to a part of him he had not known existed.

Fred's face must have shown something of what he was thinking. The explorer hammered his coconut on the ground. "I can tell! I can see that you are falling in love with this place! How do you not see, yet, why it must be a secret? How do you not see how mad it would be to gamble with such beauty?"

Fred hesitated. He could not keep it secret; it was impossible. The world deserved to know about this much beauty. The headmaster would call an assembly and call him a hero. But he had never seen anyone as utterly sure of anything as the man in front of him.

"You don't understand," said the explorer under his breath. "Speech is dangerous. Some of the most interesting things I have said I realized later I did not have a right to."

Then, abruptly, he changed tack. He became brisk.

"You said you followed my map," he said. "Does that mean you encountered the bees?"

"Yes," said Lila. "We borrowed some of their honey." She explained how Max had seen the monkeys and the ants.

The explorer nodded. "I used to do the same. Bees make good allies. I used to get the tobacco pouches made specially, by a man in the Burlington Arcade. I spent a lot of time in those parts of the jungle, but it doesn't do to be without tobacco for too long, and you can't carry too much on your person without attracting more attention from jaguars than is practical. I have tobacco pouches stationed across that whole sweep of the river. By the way, did you meet my dolphins?"

"Yes!" said Fred. "We didn't know they were yours."

The explorer hiccuped. "They're good creatures, dolphins," he said, his voice tripping over itself. "I used to feed them sardines. I worry it was a mistake, though. They trust too easily. It's a mistake, to trust too easily."

"And then there was a fire," said Lila. "A bad one. And so we came here. We thought it was the least-mad risk."

"That's exactly it!" The explorer was becoming emphatic; he "emphasized" some of the cachaça over Fred's knees.

Fred tried not to laugh.

"Take risks!" said the explorer. "That's the thing to do. Get to know what fear feels like. Get to know how to maneuver around it. But!" He paused to drink again.

"But?" asked Lila.

"But make sure the risks you take aren't taken to impress someone else."

Fred frowned. It sounded like the kind of thing the masters said at school.

"That's the way people end up with jaguars chewing at their collarbones, and nobody to love them for it." He wiped his eyes, and stared up at them.

"Risks, jaguars," said Con. "Noted."

"I took a risk once. I loved someone. Two people. A woman. And we had a child. Did you know?"

"We didn't know, no," said Lila gently. She exchanged a glance with Fred.

"I lost that gamble. I lost them." He set down the coconut and closed his eyes in a long, exhausted blink. "But I am glad to have made the wager."

"Did you . . . ," began Lila.

"I loved like I was unhinged," he said. His voice was rough. "I came at love like a child making 'up' arms. I worked out how to blink her name in Morse code." He gave a drunken grunt of laughter. "I was very young," he said. "People do not tell you that love is so terrifying. It is less like rainbows and butterflies and more like jumping onto the back of a moving dragon."

Fred hesitated, wordless, but wanting to say something that would be large enough to meet the taut pain in the man's face.

Before he could say anything, the explorer drank again, finishing the coconut in two immense gulps. "Do you all do nothing but stare? I thought children gamboled. And frolicked. Do some golicking! Frambol!"

Fred looked at the others. He had no idea how to gambol. He believed it involved running in circles with your arms in the air and lifting your knees as high as they would go, which was not, he thought, something that seemed sensible in the circumstances.

"I don't think we're really the frolicking sort," said Fred.

"Disappointing," said the explorer.

"Are you . . . drunk?" asked Con.

"Of course not." He belched, reproachfully. "I'm just . . . just . . . perhaps the world itself *is* 'drunk.' The jungle is a little more blurred than usual."

"I think that stuff must be strong," said Fred.

"That is impolite. I resent the implication."

"Sorry."

"Good," the explorer slurred. "I like people best when they're silent or sorry."

"Do you need—," began Lila, but he closed his eyes and turned away from them.

"My head aches. I can't look you in the voice. I shall sleep now." He lay down on the stone ground and closed his eyes. A noise like a motorcar began to come from somewhere deep within his chest. Moving on the tips of their toes, the children returned to their own fire.

As the dark spread over the city, a swarm of mosquitoes appeared. One of them got caught inside Fred's nose and bit his nostril.

"Is there a way to get rid of the mosquitoes?" said Con.

"I think smoking keeps them away," said Lila. "Some of the men my parents work with do it."

"I heard that smoking makes you less hungry," said Con.

"We could try," said Fred, scratching his nose.

He rolled up leaves, and Lila filled them with shredded grass and lichen, and Con lit them.

"Is this like real smoking?" gasped Lila.

Hot acrid smoke billowed into Fred's eyes. "I've never tried. Does smoking taste a bit like a garden died in your face?" he said.

"I think so," said Con. "From the smell."

"Then I suppose yes," said Fred. He discreetly put his cigarette out inside a big, empty snail shell. It didn't seem worth the feeling that his tongue was about to drop out of his mouth.

Fred looked at the two girls, who were both spitting disgustedly into the fire. He'd never really known any girls his own age, but both Lila and Con could spit as far as any boy at school. Their spit had commitment, and impact. He saw them grin at each other in the fire light.

It was a peculiar night, that night. Fred's thoughts kept returning to the man lying asleep by the fire at the other side of the ruined city square, and to his lost son and wife. The explorer was so alone, living with only the green and the birds and the endless jungle. But, Fred thought, it wasn't as if he was so much less alone himself. The thought made him shiver.

He felt something touch his ankle. He jerked away, thinking of tarantulas, but it was a hand: Con's hand, gripping his ankle in her sleep. He hesitated. Then he reached down and pressed down with his thumb on hers. He hoped the touch said, *We'll be all right. It will all be right.* It is hard to be specific, with thumbs.

But it must have worked a little, because she grew still, and her breathing became heavy and regular. Lila muttered in her sleep. Baca lay entangled in her long dark hair. Fred looked up at the vine roof above him, scanning it for snakes, and then, his flint tight in his palm, he allowed himself to close his eyes.

Fishing in the Dark

THE EXPLORER HAD NOT MOVED BY THE time the sun rose. He lay, snoring, where they had left him, a beetle perched on his chin.

Max woke up first, and kicked Fred in the crotch as he scrambled to his feet. Max scratched himself all over and then went running across the stone square, shook the explorer's shoulder, and sat down on top of him.

The explorer startled awake, and Fred flinched, remembering what the man had said about his startle reflex; but he merely looked mildly, politely appalled.

"Can I eat this?" Max asked. He thrust a handful of grasses into the explorer's face.

The explorer shifted Max gently onto the ground, sat up, and began to blow on the fire. "No, you can't," he said.

"You didn't even look!"

"The chances that the answer is yes are so slim." He looked up. "That's poisonous. No."

"Definitely poisonous or only maybe?"

"Definitely."

"Oh. And this?" He held up the explorer's chin beetle, which had fallen to the ground.

"You could eat that," said the explorer. He gently took the beetle from him. "But the Max of two hours from now would not thank you. As a rule of thumb, it's best not to eat things that are still moving."

"But I'm hungry. It's only moving a tiny bit."

"I would still emphatically discourage it."

"What does that mean?"

"It means no."

"Oh."

Max lay down on his back. He didn't cry, but his face looked blank, and older than it should be. Quietly, under his breath, he began to sing to himself in Portuguese.

Fred scraped some dew from the leaves above him and used it to clean his face. He looked over at Max— properly looked—for the first time in days. The boy was growing thin, and his cheekbones stuck out under his eyes. Lila had worked hard to make him look cared for and clean, but he had a snail trail of snot across his face and green dust in his eyebrows.

The explorer, too, was looking down at Max. His face was shaping itself into peculiar expressions; his eyes were bright, and his mouth tight.

Abruptly, he rose to his feet. His voice was brisk—artificially, unconvincingly brisk.

"What are you all sitting about for? Time is precious! Shouldn't you be preparing for your journey?"

"But how, exactly? We don't know what to do!" said Con. Her voice was almost a whine. Lila shot her a look.

The explorer's expression was very dry. "If you have a preference for surviving, you'll need to know how to spear fish. There have been expeditions when the men and I survived on fish for half a year."

Max's face lit. "Fish? Right now?"

"Tonight. There's a small lake not far from here."

"But I'm hungry now!" said Max.

"It needs to be dark. You can spend the day making spears."

"I tried that," said Fred. He slapped away a mosquito. "But the vines I used to tie the flints on kept breaking off."

"Vines?" The man looked shocked. "You don't use vines to secure a spear! That would be like using packing tape to build a steam train. Idiot boy! You use intestines. Where are the guts from your bird?"

Con pointed to the jungle, where they had buried the intestines and other rejected bits at a safe distance.

"Dig them up, and heat them over the fire, and use them as string." He made a winding gesture, as if tying a knot. "And don't bother me until then."

He turned abruptly—they were getting used to it now—and strode away, toward the far end of the piazza, toward the tangle of vines that cut off the corner of the square from sight.

They dug up the intestines. They were not a pretty sight, and being buried hadn't improved them. Con washed them in a half-coconut and Fred and Lila began laying them out on the stones, trying not to look too hard at the semitranslucent tubes.

Max tugged at Lila's ankle. "Lila! Did you hear that?"

"What?"

The air was silent, barring the constant whir of the insects in the trees above them. Then Fred jerked his head around: It was that same roar he had heard before, choking through the air.

"It's coming from there—from behind the vines," he said. "I'm going to see."

"No!" said Con. "He said, 'Don't bother me,' and I happen to think if a person wears claws for cuff links, you should do what he says."

"But what if he's being eaten?" said Fred. "Surely then it doesn't count?"

Lila shook her head. "I agree with Con."

Con looked around in surprise. "Really?"

"Whatever it is, he doesn't want us to know; and we can't afford to make him any more angry." Lila turned with unexpected firmness toward the fire. "Let's make those spears."

Reluctantly, Fred sat down. The morning was a sticky one, and nobody smelled better by the end of it. The intestines weren't easy to empty, and the process of heating them over the fire to harden them felt unexpectedly medieval.

"This is not how I pictured fishing," said Con. "I thought it was all old men sitting around on riverbanks telling people to be quiet. Like river librarians."

Fred opened his mouth to reply, but the guts dripped and spat hot fat at his teeth, so he shut it again.

He wondered if his fingers would ever lose the faint

scent of dead bird. But by the time the sun began to set he had a long-handled spear, with a flint glinting in the light. Lila's spear was strong and straight, but the wrapping around the flint had gone awry where Baca had tried to get involved in the process and covered himself in grease. Con's spear was the neatest. Her hands were competent and controlled, even with bird guts.

Fred went in search of water to wash the grease off his arms. Some of the stones had hollows in them that had collected enough rainwater to wash a small patch; he moved from stone to stone across the citadel, gradually shedding the worst of the burnt-grease smell. As he came back to the stone bedroom, he heard voices.

The explorer was kneeling on the ground, bent over his pith helmet. Lila crouched next to him.

"You have to be gentle with his knees and elbow joints." The explorer was speaking, his voice low. "They're still very fragile at this age."

Lila nodded. "I know." She reached into the pith helmet. "I can feel it, when he moves; they're so light, like seagull bones."

"Make sure you check under the armpits for parasites. There."

Baca's head reared up over the edge of the pith helmet, and he let out a wail of protest.

The explorer gave something approaching a smile. "He's being unnecessarily dramatic; the water's good for him. Now, hold him by his forearms."

"Like this?" Lila lifted Baca from his bath, dripping, his legs dangling.

"Yes. Check his stomach for ticks."

Lila checked, brushing her fingers over the sloth's belly, her eyes squinting with care. "There's nothing." Baca's fur was plastered against his skull, and his eyes were wide with the affront of it; he gave a squawk as he hung from Lila's hand.

"Now you need to dry him."

Swiftly, Lila unbraided her hair. It fell in an uneven wave to her waist. She lifted the sloth into it, and rubbed him gently. Baca snuffled among the deep brown curls. Fred saw Con, inside the stone room, give the ghost of a smile. Max was half-asleep, his head on Con's lap.

The explorer raised his eyebrows. The tip of his mouth lifted half an inch. "I doubt that particular strategy would be suggested in veterinary college. But good."

The sun was dipping over the top of the statue of the panther. The explorer looked up and saw Fred watching. He sprang to his feet, as if embarrassed to be caught mid-kindness, his bad leg catching on his good one, suddenly brisk again.

"Right! Are you ready to go? You each need to take some fire with you—the fish eyes shine red in the light. Find slow-burning wood: something dense."

They set off in single file through the dark trees, each carrying a burning branch. Baca rode, still slightly damp, inside Lila's shirt.

The explorer moved without a single rustle; the rest stumbled behind him, stubbing their toes on unseen roots. A branch whipped in Fred's face and the leaves blackened in the flame of his torch, but the wood was too green to catch fire.

"Don't burn down the jungle, please," said the explorer, without turning around.

Fred found to his surprise that the dark no longer seemed threatening. It still made his skin tingle, but the pitch-black shadows under the trees no longer bit at his stomach in the same way. The change had been so slow he hadn't felt it come.

"There are ant mounds everywhere here," said the

explorer. "Nothing too bad—the only dangerous ants are the bullet ants—but you don't want to disturb them if you can help it. I was attacked by a colony once, when I was asleep. It looked like my whole body was covered in warts."

"Oh," said Lila. "Wow."

"Quite. Not good for the morale."

They went in a new direction, northwest, down a steep incline. Every time their branches burned down to their hands, they pulled new ones from the trees and lit them. Twice, Fred lost his footing and slid until he came up against a tree. Max tripped, ate a mouthful of mud, and they had to pause until his screaming died down enough for him to walk on. Lila tried to comfort him. The explorer turned away and studied a dung beetle with angry intensity.

The lake, when they came upon it, was larger than Fred had expected. The trees that grew all around it had spread their roots under the water. The explorer took off his shoes and waded in, knee-deep.

"Come on, quickly," he said. "What are you waiting for?"

Fred followed him into the water, feeling it soak his shorts, and praying there was nothing in it with teeth.

The lake was pure black, except where his burning torch cast a yellow light down through the water to the mud and stones of the lakebed.

In the glow of the flames, red pairs of lights flitted and flashed under the surface of the water. Max laughed, delighted.

"The bigger the eyes," said the explorer, "the bigger the fish. Move slowly toward them. Hold your torch close to the surface. You lower your spear as slowly as you can into the water, and then, at the last moment, you jab. Jab fast. Don't jab your own feet. Now split up."

Lila and Con exchanged skeptical glances. They moved off across the lake, but they did not split up. Their breath was audible. It was hard to tell in the dark, but Fred thought they might have been holding hands.

Max reached out and took Fred's hand. His palm was warm and sticky.

"Let's fish!" Max said.

Fred fumbled, trying to arrange his spear properly while keeping the flame away from his face.

"If I give you the torch to hold," he said to Max, "will you try not to burn my hair off with it?"

Max took the burning branch. "Maybe," he said.

The spearing was harder than Fred had expected. The spear was thin and supple in his hand, but every time he brought it down over a fish, the fish had gone.

A swarm of mosquitoes passed over them—Max sneezed and waved his burning branch overemphatically.

"Max! I think I'd better take the branch."

"No!" cried Max. "No, no, no! It's mine! I'll be careful!"

A spear suddenly flew past them, inches from Fred's chest, and landed in the mud of the lake, its tip vibrating out of the water.

Fred jumped. Max gave a yell, rocked backward, grabbed at Fred's knees, and the two of them toppled backward into the shallows. The branch extinguished. Fred sat up, spitting water, and looked around for Max.

The explorer strode past, picked up Max with one hand, flipped him upright, and set him down on his feet.

"Are you all right?" Fred asked Max.

"I'm wet!" wailed Max. "I don't want to be wet."

"But otherwise?"

Max's face rippled, as he debated whether or not to cry. He hesitated, then: "My underpants are soggy. But I'm all right."

The explorer picked the spear out of the mud from where he'd thrown it. "Good boy," he said to Max. On the end of the spear was a fish as big as a man's thigh.

"Breakfast," said the explorer. "Come here, Fred, and learn how it works. Max, stay on the shore and guard the fish. Here, I'll give you a torch." The explorer strode to the nearest tree, pulled down a branch, lit it with his own, and handed it to Max. "Hold it away from your eyebrows."

"Should Max be left with fire?" asked Fred. "He tends to eat things."

The explorer turned to Max. "Boy, do not eat the fire, or any other part of the world surrounding you, do you understand?"

"Yes," said Max. He was sniffing the fish.

"You see? He understands," said the explorer. "Come on."

Fred wrung the water out of his shirt and waded into the lake to stand near the explorer. The man seemed to be in a good mood. Fred risked a question.

"When you go out into the trees—"

"Yes?" The explorer waded farther in, the water lapping up to his thighs. Fred followed. The black water closed over his waist.

"What are you doing there? You're gone all day—but you don't come back with food. Are you hunting?"

For a long time the explorer did not answer. Instead, he stared down into the lake. He was so still that Fred wasn't sure if he was breathing.

"There. See?" The explorer pointed down at the murky water and the submerged roots.

Fred could see nothing: only floating leaves and the moon.

The explorer's arm moved so fast that Fred didn't see it start or stop, but suddenly there was a long thin fish flapping on the end of the spear.

"*Acestrorhynchus,*" he said. "Needle jaw. Tastes like pike. Lots of bones, but delicious."

He took a length of twine from his pocket; it had a thin flint, sharp as a needle, tied to the end. He threaded the fish onto the twine.

"You asked what I do during the days," he said. "I'm fixing the thing I broke." Then he pivoted on his heel and swept the subject away with a gesture. "Look, see how I grip it? Get the spear less than a thumb's height above the fish before you stab down."

Fred stood hunched over the water. Red eyes glinted in the dark. He stabbed many rocks, some leaves, and his own ankle. Then, astonishingly, he felt the tip hit a fish. The first stab hit only the tail fin, but the fish was slowed, and Fred stabbed again, frantically, until he felt the flint meet flesh.

"I think I caught something!" He held his spear up to the light. On the end something wriggled; it wasn't large, but it was indisputably a fish.

"Wolf fish. They call it a *traíra* in these parts. Put it in your pocket," said the explorer.

Fred checked to see if he was serious, but the explorer didn't seem to be in a particularly jocular mood, so Fred put the fish in the pocket of his school shorts. Its eyes stared up at him like a gym teacher.

He waited for a moment, rinsing the fish blood off his hands, before he dared try again. "What are you fixing?"

The explorer waded deeper into the lake, up to his waist. He seemed to find it easier to speak here, in the dark. "I was on a reconnaissance mission; I was flying, looking for any sign of life below. I was circling the city, trying to work out whether there was anything to see, and my wretched engine failed. I crashed through the canopy. There was a fire, and it killed a lot of the foliage."

"What happened to the plane? Could you salvage it?"

The man's eyes flicked to the water, and he stirred his spear in the weeds.

Fred tried again. "Is that what made the hole in the trees?"

"In the canopy, yes. But the canopy was there for a reason. Whoever built this city had planted the trees so that their leaves interlock; you can't see the city from above. You could stand on the mountaintop and look down and all you would see is uninterrupted green."

"How long ago was it made?"

"I don't know. With a city so entwined with the jungle around it, it's hard to be certain about a date. A hundred years, at least, probably several hundred more. It will take at least fifty years to a hundred for those trees to grow again. I've cut down the burnt trees where I can, and tried to replant in the same places—"

"I saw! There are new shoots—down the middle of the square—"

"Precisely—but as you can imagine, cutting down a tree without a saw is not a relaxing pastime. It has taken time. Until the trees grow, I need to fix the canopy. I'm building a dust sheet of sorts, of palm leaves and vines to cover the gaps I made. An invisibility cloak."

"Is that what you do when you leave during the day?"

"Exactly. It's slowish work." He stabbed, brought up a fish, and threaded it onto the twine. The firelight cast the cuts and scars on his hands into sharp relief. "I'm erecting new portions every month or so. I've fallen out of the trees more often than is ideal. But it will be a green roof, a living protection for the ruins."

"But a protection from what?"

"From people surveying the land from the air," he said shortly. "From people looking for El Dorado. From people looking to pack places like this into parcels of stone and sell them to curious ladies and gentlemen in Chelsea for the price of a bus driver's yearly wages. From people exactly like me."

"Like you? But you're saving it!"

"No. I am undoing my own harm. But God knows what I might have done when I was younger. I was hungry to have my name in black capitals on the front page of the *Times*."

He glanced sideways at Fred. Fred shifted uncomfortably and looked very hard at the water.

The explorer stabbed again. This fish was still writhing hard, and he had to smack it against his shoe to kill it; perhaps it was this that made him flush red in the firelight.

"Europeans have said cities like this were impossible. Europeans never believed in a place like this—they believed the jungle could never have supported such numbers. They said it was too infertile, called it a 'counterfeit paradise.'"

He paused, staring unseeingly at the fish on the string. "The tribes that the Europeans met were so small—people believed there could never have been great sweeping cities. They didn't realize the tribes they met on the river were small precisely *because* they were more readily found by men like me—because European diseases were killing so many of them. Measles, influenza. God knows I have seen enough of that. This place does not need more people like me." A deep-red anger spread down his neck to his arms.

Fred didn't move; he only listened, harder than he had ever listened to anything in his life.

"My wife was born in a village in the jungle. We were young—barely twenty. She breathed the jungle, wore the jungle. She died, from measles, soon after our boy was born." His voice was flat. "She caught it from a troop of Englishmen. Amateur explorers."

"And your son? What happened to your son?"

"He would have turned four the week after he died.

Cholera." The explorer stared at the dark. "This land could, once, have supported millions of lives. And one day the world will know that. The time will come, I hope, when the world values people as much as it values land. But for now, we do not need more men in pith helmets marching through the jungle toward us."

He looked back down the path they had walked. "Neither the people who pass through the city nor the city itself would be safe."

Fred's blood was moving faster than usual through his body. He wanted to speak—to say something that would stop the explorer from looking so fierce and so lost—but his voice wouldn't come.

"Which is why"—the man stabbed again at the opaque water, but this time he missed, and there was a shake of passion in his hand—"I ask again that you swear not to tell anyone about this place. I ask it with every ounce of my heart."

Fred was glad it was dark, glad that he could not see the explorer's face, nor the explorer his. "I swear I won't." He thought, how can you make someone see that you weren't lying, that you meant it? "I'll never tell," he said, louder. "I swear!"

The explorer bowed his head. "Thank you, Fred."

"I didn't understand before! I hadn't thought—I mean, I thought it was simple."

"Extraordinary things are rarely simple."

"But if you're right about what would happen—if you're sure—"

"I would never dare say I was sure. But I believe I am right. I believe it enough to swear by it."

"Then I swear too."

The explorer gave a sigh; it sounded of things that Fred could not untangle. "Thank you."

"I'll die before I tell," said Fred. "I'll explain it to the others. And I'll never say a single thing about you."

"Me neither," said a voice. "You're *my* explorer! I don't like to share." Fred jumped. Max had waded back into the lake, still holding the torch, and was standing directly behind the explorer, rib-deep in water, preparing to hug his knee from behind.

The explorer reared away, startled by the boy's hands.

"Good God! It's best not to show affection when you're holding a naked flame, child," he said gruffly. He ruffled Max's hair.

Max giggled, and waded through the shallows toward Lila and Con, singing a song whose lyrics seemed to be composed entirely of the word "fish."

The explorer handed Fred his spear. "Here. Try with mine. It's lighter."

"But what will you use?"

"I don't, technically, need a spear." The explorer crouched low, chest-deep in the water, and lowered his arms up to the elbows. One hand flashed out through the water. There was a certain amount of thrashing, and then the explorer held up a fish, the size of his forearm, clasped in both hands. Its scales shone in the moonlight. "The only downside of doing it like this," he said, "is sometimes they turn out to be piranha, and that can be awkward."

Fred thought of his father, back home, wrapped tightly in his pinstripe days.

"I wish you were my father," he muttered, so quietly that the explorer could choose not to hear.

The explorer turned, his eyebrows high. "I would not wish that. I did not excel at the job," he said sharply. "And, Fred, it is possible your father will surprise you. It is in the nature of fathers; they are not as predictable as they seem."

"He is," said Fred. "I wanted—" He stopped, but the darkness made it easier to speak. "I wanted to tell him about this place. I thought he'd be proud."

"I am sure your father is very proud of you already," said the explorer. He was looking down at the water, half listening.

"No, he isn't!" Fred glared at the man's back. "It's simple—he'd rather my mother had never had me, then she wouldn't—"

"It is *not* simple, Fred." The explorer turned and looked him full in the face. "You must stop saying that word. Cut it out of your vocabulary. Almost nothing in life is simple."

Fred sighed. He was disappointed in the explorer. "Adults always say that."

"It remains true. The world is larger than any human imagination; how could it ever be simple?" He ducked suddenly underwater, his whole body disappearing under the black surface, and came up with something resembling an eel in his fist, which thrashed against his chest. He went on as if nothing had happened. "A man can love and fear the responsibility that comes with love. A secret can be at once selfish and necessary. Truth is as thorny and various as the jungle itself."

He turned to crouch in the water again. Then, suddenly, he froze.

He didn't raise his voice; he didn't need to. "Max.

Fred. Quick. Out of the water. Con. Lila. Get out of the water."

Fred twisted to look around. "Why?"

"Out!" His voice grew louder.

Con and Lila started wading toward them. "What's happening?"

"Move faster!"

The explorer sprinted through the shallows, his bad leg dragging behind him, grabbed Max around the waist, knocking Max's torch into the water, and strode in vast uneven steps back toward the bank. Fred ran after them, tripping over submerged roots; Lila pulled Con along through the mud.

The explorer dropped Max on the ground; he landed headfirst, but Lila scooped him into her arms before he could start screaming. The explorer turned, spear raised, to face the lake.

"What's wrong? What did we do?" asked Con.

"Nothing." Now that the children were out of the lake, he sounded entirely placid. "We're leaving."

"What is it, though?"

"See those eyes? They shine red, like the fish. There, at the far side of the lake?"

Lila swallowed. "Is that . . . what I think it is?"

Her eyes must have been sharp; Fred could see only a flash of red and a gray shape.

"Caiman," said the explorer. "It's an old one. Maybe eight feet long. Probably not interested in any of you. But." He didn't finish the sentence.

"Have you ever been bitten?" asked Con.

"A few times. Come. We might as well leave rather fast." The explorer tossed Max up into the air, grabbed hold of one of his ankles, and threw him over his shoulder.

"Follow me, you three. Put your feet where I put mine." Max, hanging over the man's back, foraged in the man's pocket.

"Fred," whispered Max, from upside down. "I have to tell you something."

"What is it?"

"I ate a tiny bite of the explorer's fish. While I was waiting. I was hungry." He held out the fish, which had his finger marks pressed into it. "Is that all right?"

Fred looked at the creases in Max's anxious face. "Yes," he said. He tried to sound as serious as he could. "I wouldn't do it again. But people do eat raw fish. I don't think you need to panic."

"I won't die?"

"No. In fact, I think maybe, in a very peculiar kind of way, we're all safe. For now."

The explorer twisted to look at Fred, almost smacking Max's head against a tree.

"Yes, you're safe," he said. "Or, rather," he clarified, "you could still die out here. But if you pay attention, you will be safe from a lot of things." He stopped, turning back to look at the file of children behind him, moonlit, sweat smeared. He shook his head. "There is no way to say such things as need to be said without sounding like a cheerleader."

He did not, Fred thought, look very much like a cheerleader. Cheerleaders, he believed, wore fewer animal teeth.

"Do you see all this?" The explorer held his torch high, casting light on the trees and the sleeping birds. "You don't have to be in a jungle to be an explorer," he said. "Every human on this earth is an explorer. Exploring is nothing more than the paying of attention, writ large. *Attention.* That's what the world asks of you. If you pay ferocious attention to the world, you will be as safe as it is possible to be." He glared at them, each in turn. For once, Fred didn't flinch under the ferocity of his gaze.

"Speaking of attention, Lila," the explorer said, "your sloth is trying to eat your hair. It will give it indigestion if it succeeds."

He walked on, Max's thin ribs bouncing against his spine, carrying him home.

The Vow

NOBODY WANTED TO SLEEP THAT NIGHT. They sat by the fire, cooking the fish until it spat and sizzled, and whispering. Fred explained to Lila and Con about the canopy; about the explorer working every day to protect the great green secret at the heart of the jungle.

"We should do something," said Con, "to prove to him that we won't tell."

"Do you think he doesn't believe us?" asked Lila. Baca lay snoring in her lap, with Max curled up on her foot, his eyes closed.

"It's not that, exactly—but I think he's not the easily believing kind," said Con.

"I like that idea," said Fred. "What would we do?"

"We could swear," said Lila "We could make a blood vow, like they do in books."

"I want something more permanent than that," said Con. She looked up at the roof, through which the stars shone, silver woven through green. "I want something bigger. Something that will make all this last forever."

"I know!" Lila sat up straighter, jerking Baca awake. "We could make a mark—like a tattoo!"

"We don't have any ink," said Fred.

"But the explorer does!" said Con. "I saw it, when I was collecting wood—he keeps his most precious things he doesn't want stolen under his hammock while he sleeps."

There was a pause. Then Fred said, "If he doesn't want them stolen, I don't know if I'd want to try stealing them. He sleeps with a knife."

Excitement seemed to have made Con bold. "I'll do it!"

Even Baca looked surprised.

"Con!" said Lila. "Are you crazy?"

But she was already up and running across the square, on her tiptoes, half bent over and muttering warnings to herself as she went. Fred and Lila exchanged startled glances.

Con returned five minutes later, bearing the ink aloft.

"I did it!" she said.

"You stole it?" asked Lila, her voice full of admiration.

"Yes!" said Con, flushed with victory in the light of the fire. Then: "Sort of."

"Sort of?" said Fred.

"He was sort of awake. He sort of said we could borrow it; he said it's precious, and if we spill it, he'll put snakes in my hair. But I would have stolen it if I'd had to."

Fred grinned. "What shall we tattoo, then?"

"We could write, 'I swear'?" said Lila.

"Too complicated. It would give us too many chances to go wrong," said Con.

"Or an *X*," said Fred. "Like the one on the map."

"I like that," said Lila. Con nodded. She sharpened the tip of the penknife with a flint, and Lila burned the tip in the flames of the fire to sterilize it.

"Who wants to go first?" Lila asked.

There was a silence, a silence sharpened by the tip of the knife in Lila's hand. Then: "I'll do it," said Fred.

He tried not to let his hands shake. It was harder than he'd expected, to cut his own skin; he dug down, wincing sharply, and cut a thin line into the base of his thumb where it met his palm.

"Does it hurt?" asked Con anxiously.

"A bit," said Fred, his voice coming out tight. "But not compared to everything else." He added a second line, and dabbed away the blood. "How do you think they put in the ink?"

"I think they just drip it on," said Lila.

The ink stung, and Fred bit his teeth together, but Con and Lila were both tactfully looking away.

"There!" he said. He held it up to the firelight: a small *X*, marked in ink and blood.

Lila went next. She winced when the ink was added but said nothing. Con took longer over hers, making sure the lines of the *X* were perfectly straight. "If it's going to be forever," she said, as she rubbed in the ink, "I don't want it to be wonky."

Max suddenly jerked upright. "I want one!" he said.

"Max! I thought you were asleep," said Lila.

"I was pretending."

"Shh, Maxie. Go to sleep."

"I want one too! I want to do the secret swear!"

"No," said Lila. "Absolutely not. It hurts, and you'll

cry, and the explorer will wake up. And anyway, Mama and Papa would kill me."

"I won't cry!"

"You would," said Con.

"But it's my secret too!" said Max. "If you want me to keep it a secret, you have to let me!"

The others looked at one another. Lila sighed.

Max did cry, but he tried very hard not to. Lila took up the knife and Max screwed up his eyes and bit his lips together and drummed his feet on the ground, and though the tears trickled down his face as Lila added the ink to his hand, he didn't yell.

"Shall we swear?" said Con. "What shall we say?"

"You do it, Fred," said Lila. "You're oldest."

Fred grinned, half embarrassed. "We swear—," he began.

"Just a second!" Con threw an armful of kindling on the fire so that it roared upward toward the sky. "Okay, go."

"We swear to keep this place a secret," said Fred. "Until it's safe to tell the world about it, or until we die—whichever comes first."

"I swear," said Con solemnly. Then: "Though,

statistically, we're more likely to die before we get a chance to tell anyone, you know." But she was smiling.

"I swear," said Lila. "Always."

"Swear," echoed Max. "It's *my* city." He looked proudly down at his *X*. "Nobody gets to share it with us."

Con looked at Lila; Lila looked at Fred. The three of them grinned at one another over Max's head.

Explorer School

THE NEXT DAY WAS THURSDAY, A FULL twelve days since the crash. Fred was woken from a nightmare about a burning airplane by the vulture pecking at the back of his head. He sat up.

"Hey!" he said.

The vulture looked at him, an irate glare of disdain for the slack of a world that had failed it.

"*Heel!*" came a voice from outside, followed by a whistle. The vulture waddled out of the stone room. Fred followed.

"Good boy," said the explorer to the vulture, tussling its naked red head as if it were a dog. The fire outside the stone room had already been lit.

"Wake the others," said the explorer.

"It's only just sunrise," said Fred dubiously. "Max sometimes threatens to pee on you if you wake him up early."

"Wake him anyway. If he chooses to weaponize his urine, so be it. I've been watching you all, and there are some basic techniques for survival that you don't yet know. I'll be working late today, so you need to listen now." He glanced down at Fred's palm, saw the mark. He said nothing, but it was possible, Fred thought, that the left side of his face smiled half an inch.

"Come, hurry! Explorer school is in session."

The others emerged, rubbing their eyes. The explorer handed out pieces of meat from a gourd cut into a serving bowl at his side.

"To get home, you need to know both the river and the land. Tell me what you know."

It was hard to say what the meat was—a bird, Fred thought, though it might have been fish. He ate as slowly as he could, chewing each piece until it turned to pulp in his mouth.

"We already know the river quite well," said Con proudly. "We came on a raft."

"Describe it."

"Fred made it," said Con. She grinned at him. Her cheek was covered in mosquito bites, but her smile was very broad. "He was fanatical about it."

"What did you use?" the explorer asked Fred.

Fred described it as best he could. He tried not to sound too proud of it.

"It sounds a good design," said the explorer, and Fred felt his face burn hot with pleasure. "I went along the Rio Negro by raft from Manaus on one of my first expeditions. I used a similar model. Not as good as a dugout canoe, but quicker to make."

"What was the expedition looking for?" asked Fred.

"Various things. Some of the men were looking for a city, others for plants for a new medicine. I was just hungry to see the world. We were naïve, and clumsy. Two men died. But I loved it." The explorer began sketching a map in the dust. "You come this way— around the edge of the rapids by Dead Man's Point, and north. Water leaping up into your face, the raft trying to ride the waves the way you would a horse, and me trying to make sure that the bamboo rod I used to steer didn't jerk and impale me through the ribs. Some of the happiest days of my life."

He handed out more meat. Max widened his eyes in appeal, and was given double. Con opened her mouth to object, and then closed it again.

"You'll have to do part of the same journey I made

before you reach the city. It will be choppy. Foam and rocks. You can get thrown several feet in the air; you'll have to tie the little one on. If anyone falls overboard, you can't grab on to the raft in those waters without capsizing it."

"Really?" said Lila. "But couldn't you—"

"No," he said sternly. "The only honorable thing to do is to drown."

"Oh," said Lila.

"Oh," said Fred.

"Fine," said Con. "What else?"

"And then there are certain preparations you must make. Have you got a pen?"

They didn't, of course, but Lila took a flint and began to scratch into a piece of gray stone.

"In the forest fifty miles down from here," said the explorer, adding to the dust map, "you'll come across a kind of bee; it's absolutely minuscule and rather beautiful. It's drawn to sweat and to moisture, and it is happiest when nesting on the center of the pupil of your eye. The people there call them 'eye lickers.' Write that down."

"Eye lickers," said Lila, scratching hard. There was no fear in her face, only concentration. Baca climbed on top of her head and sat there, an inquisitive hat.

"The best thing to do is wear a bit of net over your eyes."

"Could we make netting?" asked Fred.

"That's a good question. It's one of the very few things that it is almost impossible to make."

"Could I"—Fred closed his eyes and tried to picture what the net would need to look like—"punch holes in a bit of snakeskin?"

"Well. You could." The explorer looked at Fred, nodding slowly. "In fact, that's not a bad idea. But finding a snakeskin is difficult in these parts; the vultures eat them. I have one mosquito net. It's the most valuable thing I own, I think."

They waited.

"I suppose I can cut off four pieces, and you can tie them around your head with vines."

"Thank you!" said Fred and Lila together.

"That's kind," said Con solemnly.

The explorer waved it away, frowning, unexpectedly awkward in the face of gratitude. "And then, the vampire bats." He added further lines to the map, and some spikes, to show hills. "You need to find a way to deal with them."

Con looked up. "Please, please tell me that's a joke."

"Not at all! They come in swarms—not around here—but on the other side of the mountain. You must have heard of them?"

"No!" said Con.

Fred hadn't either. But, "Lila will have," he said.

"I've never seen one," said Lila. "But their front teeth are sharper than razors, and their tongues give off a chemical that stops your blood from clotting."

"Quite," said the explorer. "It's all very impressive from an evolutionary point of view, but very frustrating from a personal one."

"Frustrating?" said Con. "Bats that eat you are *frustrating*?"

"They don't eat you, dear child. They drink you. I assure you there's a difference. When you strike around the mountain, you need to be wary of maggots."

"Maggots," said Con. The skin on her face was lurid white.

"Yes. It's unpleasant to think of yourself as the kind of person maggots choose to associate with, but there you are. There was a disconcerting moment, many years ago, when a worm worked its way out of my skin;

it poked its head up out of my body like a meerkat rising from a hole. It was extremely surprising. I'll teach you how to extract them with a thorn and some fire. Remind me."

Lila wrote "maggots" on the list and added a question mark.

The explorer looked at them appraisingly. "You should go soon. You're nearly ready."

Fred stared at him. Somehow the news did not fill him with the relief it should have. "You should go before the rains. You can fish now. Fred knows how to set a trap. With that and the tarantulas and some berries, you should survive. The maggots get worse during the rains, and the going is much slower when the ground is boggy. And there's yellow fever, of course."

"Oh, of course!" said Con. She sounded a little hysterical. "Maggots aren't enough, without a fever turning you yellow. It sounds like a proper holiday."

The explorer ignored her. "And when you get back to the city, when they ask you how you found your way, you must lie."

"We'll say whatever you want," said Con.

"And no matter how many people ask, you don't mention my name. Do you understand?"

"We don't know your name," Con pointed out. "What is it, so we know what not to say?"

The man gave a rumble, half anger, half amusement, deep in his throat. He rose and hefted the vulture into his arms. "I will be working today. If you try to come behind the vine wall again, I'll feed your little toes to—"

"To the vulture, yes, we know," said Con.

"What was the meat?" asked Fred as the explorer turned to go. "It was good."

"What? Oh, caiman," he said. "The one in the lake."

That night Max came and tugged at Fred's foot.

"Fred!" he hissed. His whisper was extremely damp. "Fred! I have bad news. I have bad feelings."

"What?" Fred jerked awake, searching for Max's face in the dark.

"I have a bad feeling," said Max. "A lot of bad feelings."

"Shh, Max. What are you scared of?"

Max's voice was whiny, but there was real fear in it. "There's something coming."

"There's nothing coming," said Fred. "You're probably dreaming about the caiman."

He listened. The forest was never still—it rustled and insects called and monkeys bellowed all night long—but it did not sound any louder or quieter than usual.

"What kind of thing?"

"An animal. It's watching us. Or a monster. I know it."

"There's no monsters, Max."

"They're watching! I heard them!"

"The animals are just living their own lives, Max. I promise. They're not interested in us."

"I can hear them breathing!"

"You don't need to worry. The only thing you need to do is go to sleep."

It was dark under the vine roof, but Fred could see that Max's eyes were wide and unconvinced, and his hair was wet with sweat. "Can I come and sleep next to you?"

Fred hesitated. Max was not a quiet sleeper. He thrashed a lot, and bit things, and farted in his sleep.

"Please?"

"All right. But please try not to bite me, okay?"

"Yes," said Max. He took a firm hold of Fred's wrist, put it in his mouth, and went to sleep.

It was just as Fred was falling asleep that he saw

the movement in the trees. He rose to his knees and crossed, keeping low, to the doorway of the stone house. He looked out over the square. Moonlight filtered through the holes in the canopy.

Something *was* watching them. But it wasn't an animal, nor was it a monster.

It was the explorer. He was sitting in a low branch, leaning easily against the trunk, knife in hand, keeping guard.

Stuck in the Mud

THEY WOKE TO RAINS SO HEAVY THAT FRED could barely see his own hand when he held it out in front of him. The explorer had left fresh fish outside their doorway, but he was nowhere to be seen; there was only the white thundering smoke of the rain. The rain filtered through the roof and dropped on their faces. They crouched, bleakly, waiting for it to stop. It did not. They grew steadily wetter.

"Let's go and hide under the statues," said Fred. "We can take the fish."

They pelted across the square toward the far end, where the four vast statues stood. Baca let out a snuffling, mewling sound as Lila ran with him, her feet sliding in the mud.

Behind the statues, up against the wall, there was a slight overhang, enough to shelter under. They crouched, all four in a line, watching the sky and scaling the fish. Fred half expected the explorer to be there too, keeping dry, but there was no trace of him.

Fred threw a stone out into the downpour and watched it disappear into the wall of wet.

"Shall we do something?" said Lila. She offered Baca a handful of leaves from her pocket. Baca turned away and licked his damp fur. "Let's go looking for food? Or we could play something?"

Fred put down the fish he was scaling. "Play what?" He was glad to stop working. The rain made the fish slippery, his hands were covered in nicks, and his fingernails were full of fish scales. His fingers, he saw, were calloused now, toughened over the past days.

"What game?" said Con. She sounded suspicious. "I only know bridge, and we don't have any cards."

"Bridge?" asked Lila.

Con looked defensive. "We don't play much at school. Or at least . . . sometimes the others did. But I'm not usually . . ." Her voice trailed off. "I don't really want to. Aren't games for babies?"

"Do you know stuck in the mud?" asked Fred. "It's like tag, only if you get touched, you freeze until someone comes and crawls under your legs to set you free."

"Out in that rain?" Con scratched a mosquito bite.

"We can't really get that much wetter," said Fred, gesturing to his shirt. It was dripping onto the fish.

"All right." Con jumped to her feet. "Let's go!"

"You're it!" said Lila to Con.

It wasn't like any game of tag Fred had played before; it was more like swimming than running. They darted in and out of statues, slipping on the wet stone. The mud churned under their shoes and spattered all the way up to their waists. Rain got in their eyes and ears and mouths, and hammered down on their hands as they tried to lunge at one another. Con ran awkwardly, with her heels hitting her bottom behind her, but her face was vivid with excitement.

"I didn't expect this game," said Con, panting, "to be so *literal.* I like it."

They ran outward, toward the trees of the jungle. Fred scrambled up two lianas to escape pursuit, one in each hand and his knees around both for balance, until Con lifted Max in her arms and he touched Fred's ankle with the tips of his fingers.

"You're stuck!" Max called. The rain hammered on his upturned face and slicked his eyebrows into shape.

Con put Max down. She doubled over. "Wait! Fred! Lila! I think I might be dying."

"What?" Lila skidded to a halt, throwing up an arc of mud.

"The side of my side! It's burning."

"Like fire?"

"Yes!"

"And it's hard to breathe?"

"Yes!"

"That's just a stitch."

"What?"

"How do you not know what a stitch is?" asked Max. "That's so silly!"

"Shush, Max," said Lila. She turned, calming Con's deep-purple blush with her businesslike nod. "It's just what happens when you run. The best thing you can do is take a fat branch in each hand and make a really strong fist around them."

"Right! Thank you!"

"Does that work?" Fred asked. "I've never heard of it."

"Yes, it definitely works." Con ran into the rain to find sticks. Lila whispered, "I don't know, actually. I just made it up. But it might, if you believe it will. That counts for something."

Con reappeared, clutching a stick in each hand, her face pink with the effort of making a fist, straining as if she were trying to lay an egg. She thumped Fred on the shoulder. "You're it!"

If ever there is a chance to play tag in the jungle in a tropical storm, it is a chance worth taking. Years later it would shine for Fred like a gold coin he carried with him.

It was the last day of light before their days tore open.

Max

THE SCREAMING WAS NOT COMING FROM inside Fred's head.

He sat up, bolt upright, and looked around the stone room. Dawn was beginning to break. Con was clawing her hair out of her eyes to look around; Lila was already on her feet.

Max was not lying on the stone floor. Max was missing.

Fred ran out into the stone square, staring around at the gray light, praying that Max would jump out from behind a tree and stick his tongue out at them.

"Max!" shouted Lila. "Maxie! Where are you?"

"Max?" roared Fred.

The screaming stopped, and the silence battered itself against his skin harder than the noise.

"Not again!" said Con. But there was no lightness in her voice.

Then Fred's stomach turned suddenly cold, full of something writhing and maniacal. "Is that him?" He pointed at the sloping walls that they had tumbled down, to the foot of a tree. There was a bundle lying at its base.

Fred sprinted to the bank, but Lila outpaced him, her legs working like fury.

Max lay in a ball. He was shaking, his spine convulsing against his shirt, and his breathing was rough and erratic.

"Max?" said Lila. "Max, are you hurt? Can you hear me?" Her hair fell over her brother's face. "Say something!"

Max moaned and shook. His lips formed shapes, but he spoke no words.

"What's wrong with him?" said Con.

"I don't know." Lila gathered up his arms and legs and little body and stumbled forward. "I don't know! Come on!" She tripped on a rock, and nearly fell on top of him.

Fred held out his arms. "Shall I carry him?"

"No!" She held Max tighter. "Where's the explorer?" she said desperately. Her eyes raked the city.

"He'll be working behind the vine curtain," said Fred.

Lila turned, shouting as she ran. "Explorer! Hey! You! Where are you?" Baca was tangled in her hair, clutching at her neck with both arms. She did not seem to realize the sloth was there.

Fred ran after her, followed by Con, who slipped in the rain that glistened on the stones, scrambled up, her knee bleeding, and sprinted faster. Fred reached the vines ahead of Lila and began to push them away, fighting through the dense wall to where he'd seen the explorer disappear. "Help!" he called. "Are you here? It's an emergency!" His voice sounded very small and thin.

The vines parted, and the explorer stared out. His face was black with anger. "What did I say to you about this place?"

"Shut up!" Lila whipped to face him, Max cradled against her chest, her fingers clawing at his skin to hold him as he shook. "Max is sick! You help my brother or I'll kill you."

The explorer's anger vanished. "What happened? Is he dead?"

Lila let out a roar, a noise the likes of which Fred had never heard. It had blood in it. Saliva flew from her mouth, and she backed away. "No! NO! Don't you dare come near him if you're going to say he's dead!"

She stood, the tallest four feet ten Fred had ever seen, the sloth still on her shoulder like a bird on a pirate king. She blazed.

"I apologize. I was startled," said the explorer. "He's not dead. Here. Give him to me."

Tears poured down Lila's cheeks as she lowered Max into the explorer's arms.

"Get a branch from the fire. I need more light."

Fred ran to fetch a torch. Lila stood over them, unblinking.

The explorer laid Max on the floor. He pulled off his shirt and made a pillow, and raised Max's head. Max muttered but didn't open his eyes. The shaking jerked his legs. He had saliva around his mouth.

"Is he going to be all right?" asked Lila.

"I feel like I've eaten a goblin," said Con. She retched and coughed. "What can we do?"

"What's happening to him?" asked Fred.

"He's been bitten."

"By what?"

"Ants."

"Ants? Oh, thank God! I thought it was a snake!"

Con let out a bark of laughter and relief. The explorer shook his head.

"A snake would be better. He must have stood on a bullet-ant nest."

"Bullet ants!" Lila let out a moan. "Aren't they—" She couldn't say the word.

"Deadly? They can be, particularly if there are allergies involved. He needs to get to a hospital. They can treat it. But only if he gets there soon."

"How soon?" asked Lila.

"He will shake for another day, and he'll develop a fever. The fever can't be allowed to last more than five days. A week at most. It will cause the brain to swell."

"So . . . so he's just going to die? That's it?" said Lila. "You're going to let him die? You can't! I'll kill you!" Her face and eyes were wild.

"No. Of course not." The morning light showed that the explorer's face was gray and suddenly ancient. "I won't let him die. Not another."

Fred thought of the explorer's face, that night around the fire, as he had talked about love.

"How then?" urged Lila.

"Let me think," said the explorer. His tone was measured.

"No! There's no time to sit and think!" said Lila wildly. "You don't care! You don't understand! We have to do something *now*!"

"I do care, in fact. I do understand." He raised Max in his arms, and began to rub his hands and feet, trying to quicken the circulation. "I told you I had a son." He stood and cradled Max against his chest. "Come. This one will not die."

"But how do we get to the hospital?" said Fred.

"You said the walk would take a month!" said Con.

"There's another way."

"What is it? Whatever it is, I'll do it!" said Lila. "Anything! *Anything*."

"You fly."

Behind the Vines

THE EXPLORER PASSED MAX TO LILA, ONE hand under the boy's head. "Stay here with him. We'll be quick."

"No!" said Lila. "Whatever it is you're planning, I need to know." She rearranged Max in her arms, clumsy with love, cradling him to her. "Come on!"

The explorer opened his mouth as if to argue, then met Lila's eyes and shut it again. He turned to the wall of green foliage.

"It goes farther back than you think," he said. "Come, push away the vines, quick."

Fred shoved aside a great armful of the lianas, some browned with age, some thick as Fred's wrist.

The vines looked too closely woven to have grown that way. Up close, it was clear they had been draped from something; they fell, uniform, an impenetrable curtain.

"Did this grow here? Or did you plant it?" panted Fred as he pulled at the vines. It felt like trying to climb through a hedge.

"I planted it, wove it, pruned it. It is worth having a secret space." The explorer pushed past Fred, pulling out his machete. He hacked through the foliage. "Almost through." He widened a space and held back the vines for Lila. She shifted Max so the boy's head rested on her shoulder, and stepped through. Fred heard her gasp.

He pushed aside the final layer of tendrils and creepers. Con followed. He stopped short.

The vines fell from the roof of a large, three-sided stone room. It was built of similar stone to their sleeping room, but with its ceiling almost intact. It was high as a cathedral, and it smelled of moss and quiet growing things. The walls were covered in vines, and something had made a nest in the far corner, a ball of grass and feathers.

And in the middle of the bare-earth floor, something shone yellow and chrome in the green light.

"An airplane," breathed Fred.

"Precisely." The explorer strode toward the plane. "Come. Quickly."

They edged forward, clumped together, Lila's arms tight around her brother.

"Here she is." The explorer thumped the side of the plane; it was small, with just two seats set one behind the other.

"But you said it burned!" said Fred.

"I did not. *You* assumed that. I said there was a fire, which is not the same thing. I was on a recon mission when she started to choke. We crash-landed through the canopy, straight onto the stone city. Saved my life. It took five years to repair her."

Very slowly, Con put out a hand and stroked the wing of the plane.

"I've been keeping the boulevard in between the trees clear of grass ever since I came—just in case. It will make a good runway." He stopped, corrected himself. "It will make an *adequate* runway. I hope."

"We're going to fly home!" said Con. Her eyes were shining.

"I am not. I can no longer fly." He smacked his wounded leg. "You need both feet to fly a plane. *You* will fly."

"You want *us* to fly a plane?" asked Fred.

"Well, not all three of you. One of you."

"No!" said Con. "Never, not possible, absolutely not! We've already been in one plane crash. Have you any idea what the odds are on surviving two?"

"What else are you planning to do?"

Con looked at Max. She looked at the plane.

"It's much simpler to fly than you think," said the explorer.

Max gave a moan and struggled in Lila's arms.

"There is enough gas for one brief lesson and the journey to the hospital. Which of you will fly? Lila? As Max is your brother, you have first rights to it."

"I can't!" said Lila. Her eyes were full of tears. "I would! But I can't breathe when I'm near heights!"

"Con?" said the explorer. "Fred?"

"Absolutely no way in the world!" said Con. "I don't want to kill us all!"

The explorer looked at Fred. Fred looked at the plane. His insides were growing hot with the hope of it and cold with fear. His fingertips began to quiver. His ears were ringing.

"I can't," he said.

"Why not?" asked the explorer. "The thing that makes driving dangerous is the other drivers. There will be no other planes."

"On one lesson?"

"You will have to learn fast."

"What if I crash?" Fred asked.

"You will have to refrain from doing so," said the explorer.

"But—"

"You have not, I notice, said you *won't*. You have said only that you *can't*. I say you can."

"Fred," said Lila. Her eyes met his. Fred had never seen a person look at once so frightened and so brave.

"All right," said Fred. "I'll try."

"Of course you will," said the explorer. "Lila and I will make Max comfortable. I'll return in an hour. I expect you to be waiting here." The explorer held out his arms to take Max, but Lila clutched him closer to her chest.

"I'm coming with you," said Con. "I could be useful. I care for my great-aunt when she's sick."

"Don't waste time," said the explorer to Fred. "Climb into the front seat and get a feel for the controls. But don't press the black button—that's the starter. I do not recommend you try to fly through stone."

And they turned and left Fred alone in the great stone cathedral with the waiting airplane.

The Green Sky

AN HOUR LATER FRED HELPED THE EXPLORER cut and pull down the curtain of vines enough to roll the plane out of the stone shed and onto the boulevard of the ancient city.

Fred climbed into the front seat of the airplane and looked through the windshield. Seat padding was sprouting up from holes in the black leather, but the inside of the plane was spotlessly clean.

"How's Max?" asked Fred.

"Sleeping. Lila is keeping him cool with rainwater."

"Is he going to be all right?"

The explorer looked serious. "As long as you can get him to the hospital in Manaus soon, yes. I hope so."

"And if—," Fred began, and stopped.

"If not, no," said the explorer shortly. There was a muscle contorting in his jaw.

It felt entirely wrong to be sitting here while across the stone boulevard Max struggled to breathe. The explorer must have seen Fred's rigid body, must have seen him shake, because his voice grew less curt.

"He will live for now," he said. "But you must get him to a doctor. So concentrate."

Fred bit down on his tongue and clenched his fists. He looked at the dials in front of him, arranged in a row, and at the joystick between his knees. Everything shone: There was not a speck of dust or greenery.

"I clean the engine every day, to keep the rust off. And I run it every now and then, to check that it's alive. Look after the things you love or else you don't deserve to love anything," said the explorer, swinging his bad leg in after his good and settling in the backseat.

"I think we heard the engine!" said Fred. "Twice. We thought it was an animal: a panther or a bear. Or a person roaring."

"Possibly. It could, equally, have been a panther; there are some in these parts."

"Why did you hide it though?"

"For many reasons. Among others, this particular plane is readily identifiable. It is well known to belong to the man I once was. For that reason I must ask you to set fire to it, on arrival, if the impact with the ground has not already done so."

Fred twisted round to stare at him in astonishment. "*Burn* it?"

But the explorer was already pointing at the dials. "These are the things you need to know. Those dials are for speed and altitude, and that spirit level shows if you're flying straight. You want the bubble in the spirit level to be in the direct center."

Fred muttered the words after him, trying to force them into his memory. "Speed, altitude."

"The pedals bank left and right."

Fred put his feet on the pedals. They were much smaller than the pedals in his father's Ford. He prodded them experimentally. Two wires running down each side of the inside of the plane shifted as he presssed the pedals.

"The joystick"—the explorer shook the backseat joystick—"goes up, down, left, and right."

Fred held the joystick. It was black, with a red button on top. It moved loosely under his fingers.

"I have one too, in the backseat, so I can take

control at any time. This wrench—like a window winder—controls the throttle: how much power you give yourself. And that's more or less it. Now, you see the button I told you not to press: the black one, on the right?"

It wasn't a button so much as an oblong, like the lid of a fountain pen sticking out from the dashboard.

"Yes."

"Press it."

Fred pressed it. His hands were shaking. Nothing happened.

"Again," said the explorer.

Fred pressed harder.

The engine gave a moan, a cough, and then roared into action. The plane shook. Fred could feel it vibrating. It added to the wild prickling of his skin.

"Do you hear that? That's the sound of life becoming!" said the explorer. His eyes were glinting a little maniacally.

Fred whispered under his breath, "Oh, help."

"Now—taking off is the easy part. You just point the plane in the direction you need to go—up through the hole in the canopy—open the throttle, pull back on the stick, and fly."

Fred's breath had given up entirely now. "What about the rest of it?" He gestured at the dials.

"I'll tell you when you're up there. We'll have to shout; if there's a wind, it'll be loud, and the intercom was one of the few things I couldn't fix. Luckily, we have no need of a radio-control tower. Now go."

Fred's entire body was metal and stone. He had to force his feet to move, pushing the left pedal to point the plane down the jungle runway.

"Now open the throttle," shouted the explorer over the scream of the engine.

"How?" Fred roared.

"Turn the winder! On your left!"

The plane gathered speed, the wheels jolting over the slabs of ancient stone.

"Pull back! Pull back!"

Fred pulled back on the joystick with all his strength. He felt the nose lift, the front wheels leave the ground, his stomach jerk, and suddenly they were hurtling straight for the top of the canopy. The sky above him was crisscrossed with green.

Fred let out a yell of fear, but the explorer pulled back farther on his own joystick, and the tail cleared the greenery of the jungle.

"It would be a good idea to open your eyes," said the explorer. "It makes piloting easier."

Fred opened his eyes. They were in the sky.

"How did you know they were closed?"

"Mine were when I first launched a plane," said the explorer. The tinge of madness in his voice was still there. "You're flying."

Fred looked down. The jungle was an infinite sweep of green: a Turkish carpet for a god. His heart was roaring louder than the wind ripping past his ears.

The explorer leaned forward and shouted in his ear. "Use the stick to turn left. You need to get the feel of the controls."

Very gingerly, Fred tilted the stick.

"More than that! You can be flying sideways without tipping the plane over. You need to feel you can take risks."

Fred pulled the joystick hard to the left. The wing dipped, and the plane swooped in the air. His stomach swooped with it.

"Less! Less than that!" roared the explorer.

A bird flew past them. The plane was headed straight toward it. "Don't hit the birds!" roared the explorer. "It's bad for the propeller!"

Fred jerked the joystick up, and the plane tilted straight up, shuddering in the sudden altitude.

"What now! Shouldn't you be controlling it?" Fred's voice sounded panicky.

"Of course not! Joystick a little forward!" called the explorer.

The plane leveled out.

"Follow the tributary to the river."

Before Fred had time to breathe, they were flying over treetops, over a flock of parrots; and then, quite suddenly, there was nothing between his feet and the Amazon River but air and a fingernail-thin tin floor.

"Oh, God," muttered Fred. The water below was a blue purple. He could see the shadow of the plane skidding along its surface.

The explorer let out a noise that sounded like a growl, a guttural sigh. "My God, it's beautiful. I'd forgotten."

The river was staggering to look at. It made every inch of Fred thrum and burn.

"It is very easy to not want to come down," said the explorer. "If planes didn't run out of fuel, I would still be up there. It's the closest you will ever come to being a bird, or a god. Now, if you've got the feel of the controls, you can try flying through that cloud."

Fred tightened his grip on the joystick. "I don't think I want to."

"You should know how. It's important."

"Can't I just keep doing this for now?"

"No! Up! Up!"

Fred pulled back and steered the nose of the plane into the cloud. The air was bitterly, shockingly cold, and wet, and suddenly the world, which had been so intricately detailed, no longer existed.

"Keep going up!" said the explorer in his ear. "Come out of the top of it."

Fred pulled back on the stick and the nose of the plane rose. They flew up higher and higher into the blue. The joystick vibrated harder under his hand. He clutched it, trying to stop it shaking.

The explorer leaned forward and roared, "Lighter touch, Fred! I know I said you can be firm with it, but you're holding it like a steak knife. Use the tips of your fingers. You gauge the wind by how the joystick shudders," called the explorer.

Fred lifted his grip. He felt the plane hum under his fingers.

"Better!" said the explorer. The wind dropped, and the roar in his ears lessened.

Fred looked down at the green world beneath. "Are you sure we shouldn't we be getting back to Max?" he asked.

"The boy is safe for now," said the explorer. His voice was sharp. "I would not be up here if there was anything I could do for him down there."

"Sorry," said Fred.

"He looks so like my boy," said the explorer suddenly. "Those eyebrows."

Fred hesitated. "You said . . . cholera?"

"It happened a lot," said the explorer. He seemed to be trying to sound matter of fact. His voice was tight; Fred could barely hear him over the engine. "I buried my gold signet ring with him, so that anyone finding his bones would know that he was mine, and that he was loved. I made myself a replacement." The plane gave a great shudder. Fred could not tell if it was the sky or the man behind him. "If an adult tells you that you will understand everything when you are older, you are being lied to. Some things, in fact, I think you never understand."

"I'm sorry," said Fred. It felt very inadequate.

"Turn left. The government cared very little at that time for its indigenous people," said the explorer. "I wanted his death to count. All that down there"—and the explorer dipped the nose of the plane to point downward—"I've made stores of plants, roots, fungus. Of things that might have saved him. The jungle can heal, if you know how. I have stores of medicine, of herbs, of information. Did you think I just drank cachaça and polished my teeth?"

"No," said Fred. "I never thought that."

The explorer's voice sank lower. Fred strained to hear him. "I would gladly have given everything I had—my life, of course, but that's so obvious it's boring. I would have burned the entire rain forest to the ground, to hold him for a single minute. When you four tumbled down onto the city floor, I would have swapped your lives for his as easily as blinking. I would gladly have watched you die in exchange for holding him once more."

He jerked the plane sideways, and Fred gripped the seat with his fingernails. "That is no longer the case. I was afraid that my heart had simply . . . run out. But it transpires that the heart has its own gas station, its own coal, its own soap. It will renew, so use it hugely." The explorer banked sharply left again, and began circling lower.

"Now, you're going to land the plane. I'll start bringing her in."

Fred murmured a swearword under his breath, followed by another. Landing sounded like the least fun part of flying: mostly because if you got it wrong, you were liable to be distributed over the world in small chunks.

"I'm going to pretend I didn't hear that," said the explorer. "I'll get you through the canopy hole, and then you will finish the landing. You want to land with your back and front wheels on the ground simultaneously. But if you can't, it has to be front wheels first; the back one is very fragile."

Fred used his free hand to bring the collar of his shirt up to his mouth. He bit down, hard. It helped keep his hands steady, though it tasted of honey and mud and dead bird.

The explorer guided the plane toward the hole in the canopy. Fred craned around to look at him. His face was concentrated, and glowing. They dipped down through the hole.

"Now take the controls!" called the explorer.

Fred aimed for the stretch of boulevard, and for the panther. As they hurtled downward, the thought of Max, somewhere on the stone below, overtook Fred, and he jerked the joystick forward and down, away from where the boy might be lying.

The front wheels hit the stone, and bounced off again. The impact threw Fred forward, and his head smacked against the dashboard. The explorer took over the controls, wrenching the plane around; it bumped once, turned, sped up, and climbed back into the air again, back out through the hole. Fred shook himself, disoriented. They were back in the sky.

"That wasn't bad!" called the explorer.

"What do you mean? It was terrible! I nearly killed us," shouted Fred.

"Not bad for a first try. The instinct is to push down with the stick, to get the nose on the ground." The explorer sounded calm. "But you have to pull backward, and up. You can practice that with the plane, later, on the ground. You need to get the instinct into your fingers. Now I'll loop us and come in again."

This time as they approached the stone, Fred pulled the joystick up. He held the stick steady in his hands; the nose was tilted too high to see the ground through the windshield, so he leaned out the side, peering ahead, his heart screaming in his chest.

The plane touched down, rose again, bumped, and

suddenly it was speeding along the stone floor toward the wall. The wall seemed to be coming up very fast.

"Slow! Slow to a halt! Good!" The explorer reached forward and pulled back the throttle and took over the controls. "Good." The plane stopped.

Fred sat in the front seat, sweat coursing down his face, both hands gripping his knees. It was astonishing, he thought. It was like nothing else on earth. He felt wobbly, uncooked.

"Now. What was that word I heard you say in the sky?" said the explorer sternly.

"Sorry," said Fred.

"Where did you learn that word anyway?"

"School."

"Pilots never swear. It makes them look panicked. Kindly remember that, and never let me hear you swearing again, in any circumstances."

"Sorry," said Fred again. But it was difficult to feel truly sorry, difficult to feel anything except the roar in his ears and the bite of adrenaline in his blood.

"But well done. That was a landing you should be proud of."

Fred shook his head. "I bounced."

"But you rescued it. That's the only part that matters."

Waiting for Dawn

LILA SAT WITH MAX'S HEAD IN HER LAP AS HE tossed and moaned. Baca rested on the boy's stomach, breathing softly into his skin. Lila's eyes were red, and she'd bitten her lip so many times it was bleeding.

As the evening started to grow blue, Fred could feel his nerves begin to crackle with terror. Max looked so thin, lying in the firelight, as if a single jolt from the airplane might kill him. He sat counting Max's breaths until at last he could take it no longer. He jumped up and went in search of the explorer. He found him bending over the plane's engine, a burning torch in one hand for light.

"You'll have to take off as early as you can tomorrow," said the explorer. "Max is lucid but burning hot. Follow the river. If you get lost, there's a compass in the plane. Con will be your navigator; she has a memory for topography. The river will take you to Manaus; the city's built right on the banks of the river. You can't miss it; there's a vast opera house, with a glass dome roof and pink walls. The roof catches the sun, and you can see the shine of it from miles away. But if you run out of gas before you reach the city—and I must warn you, you probably will—fly inland—there will be some cattle ranches, with open fields. Land in the smoothest field you can find. Remember: front wheels first."

"Front wheels first."

"And the others should be heads down low, behind the seats, and covering their necks with their arms."

"What if I forget, though? What if I go crazy and panic?"

"I think it is very unlikely you will do either."

"What if I do, though?"

"You won't. Fred, I may be eccentric, but I am not mad." He looked at Fred: the kind of look that on a clear day could see through your chest cavity to your heart. Fred backed away. "I wouldn't ask you to do this if I weren't absolutely sure you are capable of doing it."

Fred twisted his fingers. "Are you sure you can't

come with us? I mean—your leg doesn't stop you climbing trees."

"Insolent child," said the explorer. He reached into the engine and tightened a bolt. His wrench was carved from bone. "But no. You wouldn't all fit in the back."

"We could do it in two shifts!"

"There is only enough fuel for one journey. One way, Fred. And the plane would not take off with the weight of five people; I would have to leave one of you here."

"I could stay here! With you!" he said, wondering as he said it if he meant it.

"You could not, Fred. There are people at home who need you."

"Adults don't need children."

"Yes, they do!" He looked suddenly so fierce that Fred took a step backward.

"You said children are undercooked adults."

"I know. I had forgotten things I should have never forgotten. Trust me. Your father needs you more than you know."

Fred said nothing, just stood staring at the plane, holding himself still.

"Fred. Listen to me. Even if I could fly Max myself, it would mean I'd never get back here. They would recognize me; they would recognize the plane. There would be questions, and interviews, and newspapers."

"Why? Why would there be interviews? Is it because—is it because your name is Percy Fawcett? Or John Franklin? Or Christopher Maclaren? Are you one of them? The lost explorers? You are, aren't you?"

"John Franklin would be more than a hundred and fifty years old if he were alive," said the explorer mildly. "That's rather unflattering, Fred."

"But you've got to be one of them!"

"I told you: I've been alone so long I have no need for names."

"You're just a coward! You're scared to leave."

"I do not want to leave, certainly. And that is my choice, Fred."

Fred made a face.

"I know. But believe me. This is where I am happiest."

Fred found himself swept with an unexpected wave of fury. He fought back the many unforgivable things he could have said. "You don't seem all that happy," he mumbled.

"'Happy' is a peculiar word. It's one of the few words

that make me sad. I should have said: This is where I feel most honest."

"That's insane!" Fred felt himself grow hot. Every inch of his skin was raging, including his gums.

"Why are you angry, Fred?"

"I'm not!" He glared at him full in the face. "I'm scared, all right?"

"Of course you are. But you've been scared all along, and you've kept going."

"But that was different!"

"Why?"

"The others did everything with me. The raft, and the food, and everything."

"It has to be one of you. Why not you?"

"If I mess this up"—he didn't say, *If we die,* but it was there, unspoken—"it will be my fault. This is worse."

"Then you will make the decision to steer toward fear. I think you can. I think you were built to pursue the things you are afraid of. Fear is a panther. Humans are stronger than panthers. You fight it, tooth and claw. But you don't stop when you're tired. You stop when the panther's tired."

Fred nodded. Then, just to check, he asked, "Do you mean metaphorically, or—"

"Metaphorically, yes. Although also sometimes—in the case of my leg, for instance—literally."

There was a cough behind them.

"Can I talk to you about something?" said Con.

The explorer bent over the oil tank. "Yes, of course," he said. "What's on your mind?"

Con glanced at Fred. "Alone."

The explorer didn't look up from the engine, but he jerked his head at Fred.

Fred glared at Con but turned to go. He was halfway across the city square when he heard her speak. She tried to whisper, but her voice was sharp and carried on the night air.

"I'm not leaving."

Fred turned in astonishment. The explorer was still methodically checking the engine. Fred stepped behind one of the trees that lined the central stone boulevard.

"I'm staying with you," Con said to the explorer. "I've made up my mind. Max needs to get to the hospital, but *I* don't."

"I'm afraid you're not," said the explorer. He adjusted a bolt in the engine.

"I wouldn't be any trouble. I've been saving my

food, and I can eat spiders. I've got lots of dried meat in my pockets."

"I know: I can smell it. And your face gave you away hours ago. There's a hint, and then there's an alarm going off on the ground floor of the Bank of England. Your face is a siren. I'm sorry, child. But you will be getting on that plane."

"I can't! I just can't."

"I know," said the explorer. His voice was very gentle. "But you have to."

"I'm better here. At home, sometimes, I wish people were dead."

The explorer nodded, silent. He waited.

"You don't understand!" said Con. "I wish it really hard. Sometimes I'm almost sick, I want it so much."

The explorer nodded. "That's something that the human heart does, Con. It bites. Don't let it panic you. It will pass, that specific kind of wishing."

"How do you know?"

"Between the ages of ten and sixteen I spent much of my time wishing half my class and most of my schoolmasters dead, and all of them remained indubitably, frustratingly alive. Nothing bad happened to any of them. Or—one of them, I believe, did move to Belgium. But that was as far as it went."

"But I need to stay here!" Con's face was pink. "Everything makes more sense here."

"I understand. Although, of the four of you, I rather thought you were the least keen on this place?" said the explorer.

"You're allowed to change your mind!" She was turning steadily more red: red at the ears, at the neck, rising to her forehead. "I *love* it. I've never loved anything like this! At home—it's just—it's all sit still and don't touch. Everything has a cover so I don't get it dirty. Some of the covers have covers! People want me to be ways I can't be."

The explorer nodded. "I know what that feels like."

"But if I want to scream here, I can. If I want to eat with my fingers, or climb a tree, nobody stops me. I can sleep when I want to, and I can *run* if I want to." She looked particularly defiant at the last words, as if confessing a sin.

He seemed to swallow a smile. "You don't have to go to the rain forest to do those things. They are more to do with you than with the jungle. Pay attention to the world the same way you did out here. It will change the way you feel. Attention and love are so closely allied as to be almost indistinguishable."

"Please," Con whispered.

He sighed. "You need to go home because I don't want people coming looking for you and finding you here. I cannot have people finding this place."

He squatted down to look Con in the eye. "But know this: This is the first, and not the last, of your adventures. It's not going to be easy for you. You will have to be honest, resist the urge to arrange your fears and angers at their most becoming angles. You're not one who was born to ride lightly over the world. Do you know what a lion heart is?"

"I'm not sure," she said. She was blinking hard.

"People think it means brave—and it does—but it also means a heart with claws. That's you. Con the Lion Heart."

Fred stepped into their line of vision. He coughed loudly. Con whipped around and glared, a black glare of embarrassment.

"I thought you'd gone," she said. "I didn't know you were an eavesdropper." She began to stalk away.

Fred ran after her. He wasn't sure if what he was

about to do was a sensible idea. It might, he thought, get him elbowed in the face.

"Con," Fred said, "where do you go during the holidays?"

"I live with my aunt. You *know* that," she said aggressively. Then, after a long pause, she said, "Why?"

"Well," Fred said, "it's just, we've got a spare room. And my father's always telling me to bring more friends home."

"Friends?" said Con. A flush began to rise up her neck to her ears and cheeks.

"Obviously," said Fred. "Friends."

Flight Home

LILA WOKE FRED JUST BEFORE SUNRISE. THE light was blue-gray, and her face was gaunt. She looked closer to eighty years old than twelve.

"You have to make sure he gets there, Fred," she said. She took hold of his arm and dug her nails into it, to make sure he was listening. "You don't have a choice."

Fred could feel the heat radiating from her skin, the heat of hope, and desperation, and love. "I know that," he said.

He barely had time to splash water on his face before the explorer was calling them.

"Quick, all of you!" He stood in the middle of the stone city in a patch of sun, the light shining on the scales of his signet ring. "It's time."

They gathered around the airplane, just as they had

in the airfield. It felt, Fred thought, like years ago. They were all four of them less neat now; their clothes were burnt, mud covered, fish flavored, torn. Their faces and hands were covered in mosquito bites, in scratches. They were slightly thinner, slightly rangier, slightly tougher.

Lila's hands were shaking as she took Baca and draped him over the explorer's neck. "He makes a much better scarf than monkeys do." Her eyes glittered, but she did not let a tear fall. "Will you look after him?"

"What?" said the explorer, startled. "Of course not."

"But, please! He's not old enough to be alone yet— he needs—"

"He doesn't need me. He needs you. He's yours. You rescued him, you fed him. You need him."

"But my parents—"

"Your parents will understand. They will see these are not ordinary circumstances." He placed Baca over her shoulder, as if affixing a medal. "You belong to each other."

The explorer lifted Max and laid him in the back-seat. "Comfortable?"

Max's eyes were closed and his breath was very shallow. His fingers had begun to swell.

"Not long now, little cataclysm." He touched Max's head, and turned to Lila. "He is a very loud enigma. But I am glad to have met him. Very glad."

"He loved you," said Lila. "*Loves* you," she corrected herself, blanching.

The explorer swallowed, nodded. He cupped his hands for her foot, and she climbed into the plane, cradling Max in her lap.

"Listen." The explorer looked down at Max's flushed cheek. "When you get home, tell them how large the world is, and how green. And tell them that the beauty of the world makes demands on you. They will need reminding. If you believe the world is small and tawdry, it is easier to be so yourself. But the world is so tall and so beautiful a place.

"And all of you—do not forget that, lost out here, you were brave even in your sleep. So do not forget to take risks. Standing ovations await your bravery."

Con swallowed. "But I'm afraid," she whispered.

The explorer nodded, scarred and dusty and matter of fact. "You are right to be afraid. Be brave anyway."

He held out his hand to Con, and she took it like a queen and climbed into the plane. She squeezed in next to Lila on the backseat, and together they arranged Max across their laps.

The explorer looked at Fred. Then he jerked his head toward the front seat. Fred swung up into the plane.

"Lila, hold Max steady; I'm about to shut the door." He slammed the yellow tin door of the plane shut, and fixed the catch. "And one more thing! Remember—if you learn nothing else, remember to check daily for maggots. I once had an entire colony in the crook of my elbow."

"In your elbow?" Fred's brain spun a full circle.

"Exactly so. It was a terrible blow to my vanity." He turned to go.

Fred's eyes stretched wide. "Wait!" he called. "I think I know who you—"

But the explorer was already stalking back into the jungle. Fred stared after him.

Max gave a grunt of pain and Lila bent over him. "We need to go," she said.

Fred nodded. He shook himself and set his feet against the pedals. His feet were shaking. He took a last look at the explorer.

"Ready?" he called to the backseat.

"Ready," said Con. Her jaw was locked so tightly he could hear her teeth creaking, but she managed to smile.

"Ready," said Lila. She gathered Max closer to her, and sheltered his head in her arms.

Fred glanced over his shoulder. Max lay still, breathing shallow breaths. Con and Lila were holding hands, and their knuckles were white.

Fred pressed the ignition button. The engine woke, sputtered, gave a roar like an animal.

He pulled back on the throttle and steered the nose of the airplane straight toward fear and toward home.

Another Kind of Exploring

THE FIELD THEY LANDED IN WAS A LARGE one, used for grazing cattle. It was a long field, and green as the Amazon. They bumped painfully, rose, thumped down again. The cows bellowed in terror and scattered. The front wheels shook, the back wheel bucked. There was a moment where it felt as if they would flip wing over tip, but the plane shuddered, roared, and stilled.

The cows never fully recovered.

For the rest of his life, Fred would feel gratitude when he smelled fresh-mown grass.

The rest of it was a blur. Fred and Con burned the plane by dropping a lighted branch into the engine, Lila standing well back with Max in her arms. They sat in the grass, watching the yellow wings turn red, and waited. Before long, the fire attracted a crowd. There were hoards of people shouting in languages Fred didn't know, with Lila attempting to interpret.

Then a journey by horse to a family with a motor launch, doctors, the boat ride, Manaus. A hospital for Max. Telegrams, telephone calls. A man and a woman tiptoeing into a hospital room and gathering Max and Lila so tightly in their arms they gasped for breath.

And then a huge ocean liner with a gold-walled dining room and steak and ice cream and a piano that Lila played, hesitantly, beautifully, seated between her parents with Baca chewing her shoulder, while Con and Max leaped in circles around the mirrored ballroom, scandalizing the other passengers.

Fred sat with his knees tucked up on one of the silk-backed chairs and watched them. He tried to speak sternly to his body, but whenever he thought of his father, his fingertips and knees began to quiver with nerves and hope. "Don't," he told himself. "Don't. It's an office day. He has to work. He'll send the housekeeper."

Each day the air grew cooler every hour; the smell of the sea changed from green to blue. And then, before he had time to set his thoughts into straight lines, to brush the green of the Amazon from his heart, the ship was heading toward the dock.

A row of people stood by the waterside, their fists tight, their eyes vivid with tension and longing. Fred raked them for a familiar face.

The sailors lowered the gangway, and Lila and Max let out a cry. Their grandmother stood at the barrier, stretching toward the ship; the two of them hurtled down the gangplank and were swept up in her embrace. Their parents followed, laughing. The old woman had the same wicked tilt to her eyebrows as Max.

"Con!" called a voice. Con turned, and her face flashed suddenly alight. Fred turned in time to see her great-aunt, standing upright and gaunt and shaking with emotion as she watched her great-niece descend the gangplank. Fred saw Con's aunt reach out and take hold of her wrist. She held it in both hands, as if to make sure Con was real.

Fred followed at a distance. Nobody called his name.

He stood still in the bustle of the customs shed, looking out toward the ship. He tried to still the roar of disappointment in his chest.

And then, suddenly, Fred saw his father, his suit crumpled beyond recognition, his coattails flying, running toward him, pushing aside sailors and women in elaborate hats, flying faster than any airplane.

"I thought I'd lost you," he said. He pulled him so close Fred felt his ribs creak next to his heart. "I could not have borne it. I could not."

Fred buried his face, hard, in his father's coat. He thought of the man, alone again, striding out through the jungle. He could almost hear his voice. *Every human on this earth is an explorer.*

Sometimes, "exploring" is a word for walking out into the unknown. Sometimes, it's a word for coming home.

Epilogue

TWELVE YEARS LATER

FRED PUSHED OPEN THE DOOR TO THE RITZ and strode toward the tearoom as fast as he could go without running. He ignored the excited whispers from a crowd of boys that followed him across the foyer.

Max jumped up when he saw Fred coming, and knocked over the sugar bowl. He was tall now, as tall as Fred, and his face no longer had its baby roundness; but his eyebrows still pointed upward at the ends.

"You came! We thought you might still be on your expedition!" He embraced Fred, crushing him hard around the arms.

"Fred!" Lila had grown beautiful, so beautiful that Fred always hesitated, feeling oddly embarrassed each time they met, until she grinned at him. Her wonky tooth, slightly more wonky now, was still there. She gave him a bear hug. "How was your trip? You've been in all the papers. 'A new kind of explorer,' they say."

Before Fred could answer, a voice made them turn.

"You all look so smart," it said. "You should have told me; I would have worn my ruffles."

"Con!" said Max.

As first glance, Con looked very like she had that first morning at the airfield; still with a jutting jaw, still at right angles to herself. But the blond curls were gone, as was the expression of distrust. She wore her hair in a bob, with high-waisted trousers and a felt hat that looked, just a little, like a pith helmet.

The hat, in fact, had been a Christmas present from Fred the year before. Fred's father still called the upstairs spare bedroom, Con's room.

The waitress approached, an armful of menus outstretched.

"Thank you," said Con, "but we decided what to have a long time ago."

"Could we have one of every cake on the menu?" said Fred.

"And four hot chocolates," said Max. "In honor of the grub pancakes."

As soon as the waitress had gone, Lila reached under the table.

"I brought someone to celebrate our finally being all in the same room," said Lila. "He's very, very old. The waitress might not like it, though—can you make a barrier with your coats?"

Lila lifted a bundle of gray fur from the wicker basket by her side. Very, very slowly, it opened its eyes.

"Baca!" said Fred.

"He's grown so enormous!" said Con.

"He's a very respectable old man these days," said Lila, "but he used to be such a terror."

"A very slow-motion terror," said Max.

"He kept trying to eat the covers of my biology textbooks."

They passed Baca from hand to hand; his fur was less fluffy, and he moved creakily, but his eyes were shining black and his nose was still inquisitive. He raised one slow arm and scooped up a lump of brown sugar.

Then Fred held out his hand, palm up. It was very faint now, the mark, but you could still see it.

"Still a secret?"

Lila held out her hand. "Still a secret."

Max spread his hand on the tablecloth. "Of course."

"Always," said Con.

Fred looked down at their four upturned palms; his own was still covered in burns and blisters from his last expedition, Lila's was speckled with animal scratches, Con's was stained with ink.

Max broke the silence. "Do you think he's still there?

"I don't know," said Fred. "But I'll find out soon. I'm going back to the Amazon, as soon the rains are over. I'm going to try to find it again."

"But not to take anyone else to see it?" said Con.

"No!" said Fred. "Of course not. Just to say thank you. Just to say we kept exploring."

ACKNOWLEDGMENTS

This book comes freighted with thanks to so many people. These are just some of them.

First and foremost, to my wonderful editor, Ellen Holgate. To everyone at Bloomsbury, and especially to Emma Bradshaw, world's best publicist. To my super-agent, Claire Wilson. To the great David Gale and everyone at Simon & Schuster in America.

To my brother, who reads my first drafts and is unfailingly overgenerous about them. To my parents, ever and always.

To my friends, and especially to Daisy Johnson for reading an early version. To the galvanic community of UK children's writers.

To Simon Murphy, who came with me to the Amazon and risked the piranhas.

To our guide among the caimans, Tariq Shariff, who taught me how not to die in the jungle.

And to Charles Collier, who told me to add more fire.